Jeanine Englert's lo[...]
and romance began w[...]
grandmother's books[...]
When she isn't wrang[...]
she can be found trying to convince her husband
to watch her latest Masterpiece/BBC show
obsession. She loves to talk about writing and
her beloved rescue pups, as well as mysteries
and romance, with readers. Visit her website at
jeaninewrites.com.

Also by Jeanine Englert

The Highlander's Secret Son

Falling for a Stewart miniseries

Eloping with the Laird
The Lost Laird from Her Past
Conveniently Wed to the Laird

Secrets of Clan Cameron miniseries

A Laird without a Past
The Lady's Proposal for the Laird

Discover more at millsandboon.co.uk.

A LAIRD TO PROTECT HER

Jeanine Englert

MILLS & BOON

First published in Great Britain 2024
by Mills & Boon, an imprint of HarperCollins*Publishers* Ltd,
1 London Bridge Street, London, SE1 9GF

www.harpercollins.co.uk

HarperCollins*Publishers*, Macken House, 39/40 Mayor Street Upper,
Dublin 1, D01 C9W8, Ireland

A Laird to Protect Her © 2024 Jeanine Englert

ISBN: 978-0-263-32095-4

10/24

This book contains FSC™ certified paper
and other controlled sources to ensure responsible forest management.

For more information visit www.harpercollins.co.uk/green.

Printed and Bound in the UK using 100% Renewable Electricity
at CPI Group (UK) Ltd, Croydon, CR0 4YY

To Paula Chaffee Scardamalia.

Thank you for helping me to see my stories
through tarot and for unlocking my gut
understanding of my characters. I will always
remember when I attended one of your workshops
when I was writing one of my first books, unsure of
my hero's motivation. You had us all draw
tarot cards, and I pulled the Three of Wands.
You asked me, 'Is he waiting for someone to arrive
or watching someone leave?'

Somehow, I find I am still awaiting that answer—
and I don't mind at all.

Prologue

Loch's End, Argyll, Scotland,
26th December 1745

Second son Rolf Cameron loathed goodbyes, but his life had been full of them.

Tonight would be no different.

Boisterous music filled his ears. A glorious sea of colourful gowns twirled before him as couples swirled along the dance floor in the lushly decorated, hallowed halls of Loch's End. The warmth of the crush of people celebrating his older sister Susanna's marriage to Laird Rowan Campbell was nothing short of a miracle. Now, Rolf just needed one more.

The harmonious and upbeat chords of the reel

came to a stop, and his older sister met his gaze as he stood near the edges of the ballroom. She smiled and whispered something to her new husband before she lifted her skirts and rushed from the dance floor to his side with the full bloom of hope and joy for the future flushing her cheeks.

Self-loathing gurgled in Rolf's gut. He was about to put a thistle in her revelry. Guilt niggled at him as he held a tight smile. *Steady.* He couldn't let her steer him off-course. This was his only option. He had to see them all safe. He had to subdue the threats that remained.

'Congratulations, Susanna,' he said, pressing a kiss on his older sister's warm cheeks. 'You are a glorious bride, and I could not be happier for you and Rowan. You are officially now a Campbell, although I hope you know you will always be a Cameron,' he said, unable to keep the emotion from deepening his rolling Scottish burr.

'Thank you, brother. I cannot imagine a happier day. To be wedded to the man I love with our families by our sides is more than I could have hoped for. And, aye, I know I shall always be a Cameron.' Susanna clutched Rolf's hands in her own and squeezed them briefly before letting them go.

'Then you will not be displeased when I tell you I must take my leave.'

'Leave?' She faltered, her brow furrowing. 'This celebration will continue for hours. There is no need for haste.' She smiled at him and dropped her voice. 'Unless a lady here has caught your eye?' She winked at him.

He chuckled. 'Nay. It has been some time since a woman has caught my eye, as you well know.' While he was good at finding a woman to bed if he wished to, his ability to have anything meaningful or lasting was lacking. There was far too much risk in such attachments.

'Brother,' Susanna said softly, her bright-blue eyes deepening. He shifted on his feet. He knew what was coming. 'I wish you would take some of the advice you gave me,' she continued. 'Open your heart. You cannot let fear of loss or rejection keep you trapped in the past. What happened with Joanna…'

Joanna.

His throat dried and his toes tingled in his boots. He could not think of her, not now, or he might lose his nerve. The mere thought of another loss, of losing someone else he loved, made his pulse quicken and restlessness bubble in his veins.

'Please,' he pleaded, clasping her forearm gently. 'I know you mean well, but the path you, Royce and Catriona have travelled along to build your own families may not be mine.' The idea of being so in love with a woman and losing her again terrified him.

'And, when I say I must go, I do not mean just this celebration.' The familiar pull of family tightened his chest. He knew she would not like what came next.

'What do you mean?' she asked, not following his meaning. 'You must go somewhere *now*? It is the middle of the night.'

'Aye. I must. I am headed to the Borderlands, and I need to arrive in Melrose before the New Year. I cannot waste another moment. I cannot be late.'

Susanna stilled, finally understanding, her eyes searching his. 'Are you serious? You plan to meet this stranger, this supposed antiques dealer, about Mother's letters?' she asked, dropping her voice to a whisper. 'How do you even know if he is legitimate?'

'The man is genuine. I had Royce's men investigate it for me. Bartholomew Hay *is* an antiques dealer. He owns a shop in Melrose. And the letter he provided to us...it appears to be of Mother's hand. Her writing was most distinctive—you know this—and it matches. Mr Hay claims to have more of them and additional information about our clan that is of great import. He says the letters will help protect us from Laird Audric MacDonald, but time is of the essence. I can delay no longer.'

His sister crossed her arms against her chest and frowned. 'Did he say this?' she asked.

'Nay, not exactly, not in so many words. But the intimation was there. I cannot stay and merely hope all will be well with the clan, Susanna. The safety of this family is most important to me, and I know Royce cannot leave the clan with times as perilous and uncertain as they are now, and with his wee babe on the way.'

Rolf stepped closer to her, taking in the scrutiny of her bright-blue gaze. He almost told her of the dreams he had been having, the nightly hauntings he could not explain, but he clamped his mouth shut instead. He dared tell no one—not yet, anyway. He needed to know what they meant first.

'Has brother commanded you to leave and put yourself at risk?' she demanded, pulling back her shoulders and furrowing her brow. 'I will not have it if he has done such. Where is he?' She scanned the room.

There was his older sister, protective and fierce, and he could not help but smile. He shook his head and rested a hand on her shoulder. 'Nay. It is *I* who will be disobeying Royce's orders by leaving. This is my decision.'

'And does Catriona know what you are doing? That you are taking this foolish risk in hopes of protecting her and us? We do not know if this promise of letters is even true, or if it will help us unearth the truth about our past and the intrigues our parents involved themselves in. It could be yet another ploy by the MacDonalds or some other enemy setting a trap to weaken us. We do not know who we can trust any more; you know this,' she insisted.

Rolf did not reply. He sucked in a steadying breath and felt his weight settle into his boots. 'Aye. I know all of this, but I also know that not knowing is putting us at greater risk. And I cannot have this next generation of Camerons suffering as we have. I refuse to.' His voice shook more than he would have liked, but he could not pretend he wasn't sick and tired of how the secrets of their parents' past continued to draw their blood upon them now. He wanted to protect his unborn kin, as he wished he had been protected. Enough was enough, and the agony would end with him.

Susanna nodded, her eyes softening with an understanding only one of his siblings would have.

'Have you told Catriona?' she asked again, quieter this time.

Susanna's question pricked Rolf's resolve, and his gaze cast out to see his other sister, Catriona, heavy with child, standing beside her husband and smiling with joy. This was the part of his mission he did not like. Deception was a poison he knew well, but he dared not tell Susanna the truth, so he said nothing. He despised lies. His childhood had been full of them. All they caused was rot and ruin.

Susanna clutched his hands, her gaze boring into him, and he shifted on his feet. 'You must tell her. Do not leave this place without her knowing, without her blessing, in case…'

He knew what she left out: in case he did not return.

'Blessing?' He scoffed, shoving away the thought of this being his last moment with his family. 'No one shall give me their blessing.'

Her fingers tightened around his own. 'Nay, I do. I'd have half a mind to send Rowan with you if I did not believe you would merely annoy each other to death,' she teased. Her eyes glistened with emotion in the soft candlelight.

'You are right as always, sister. I shall tell her. Your blessing has given me strength.'

He pulled her into a fierce hug. 'You have always had strength, my brother,' she whispered in his ear. 'More so than all of us, but you are loath to believe it, to believe in yourself. If anyone can find the truth and put this to rest for the sake of our family, it is you. You have a purity of heart and purpose like no other.'

The softness of her words and the way she cupped the back of his head with her open palm, as she had done when they'd been children, made his pulse jump.

Did he have such strength? Could he finally put all the chaos and carnage of his parents' lies and secrets to rest and keep his family safe?

He pulled away from Susanna before he dared answer the questions in his mind and pressed a kiss on her cheek. He set off to have one of the hardest conversations of his life. If he thought telling Susanna of his departure had been difficult, telling his other beloved sister, Catriona, would be akin to setting himself alight.

Chapter One

Melrose, Scotland,
Hogmanay, 31st December 1745

The antique wall clock chimed. Kenna Hay glared at the dark metal hands neatly stacked upon one another pointing to eleven, eager to begin the evening's celebration of a glorious upcoming New Year. Her leg bobbed up and down as she waited on the large settee in the sitting room.

'Where did you say Father had gone, Bridget?' Kenna asked their beloved housemaid.

'He didn'a' say,' Bridget replied, lifting the last of the celebratory meal from the warming oven, a fragrant currant tart that made Kenna's mouth water, before setting it delicately upon the table filled with all their favourites. The dining room had been decorated with great care. The finest of their glass-ware and plates had been set out and the utensils shone with polish. Kenna couldn't help but smile. Father had never missed a Hogmanay celebration. It was his favourite day of the year. He would love how they had transformed the small room with such a vibrant feast.

'He rushed out an hour or so ago, when you were getting dressed for the eve, as if he were afire, miss,' Bridget added. 'Said he'd an errand to attend to. Last minute sale, perhaps, or a forgotten meeting?'

'On Hogmanay?' Kenna replied, shaking her head. 'Why could it not wait?'

'Ye know yer father.' Bridget smirked and shook her head. The woman knew Kenna's father as well as she did.

Kenna smiled and chuckled. 'Aye, I do.' Bartholomew Hay was a brilliant and eccentric man prone to forgetfulness but a fiercely loyal, loving and protective father. He also had a jovial spirit, which made the idea of being late to this year's Hogmanay celebration odd indeed. In the span of a year, they had saved their family antique shop from ruin and turned a tidy profit to boot. There was much to celebrate.

Kenna's fingers were restless, and she fiddled with the drawstring on the dark-blue cloth satchel she always had secured to her waist. It had been her mother's before she'd left and abandoned them over a decade ago, since then presumed dead. The familiar tug of loss at the feel of the soft, worn cobalt fabric along Kenna's fingertips greeted her as her palm glided down, cupping the satchel. She turned the set of runes within it over and over. The rhythmic rolling of the carved stones and the sound of them turning against one another within it soothed her, as it often did…until suddenly it didn't.

A stone settled between her thumb and index finger in the bag, and she stilled. Keeping it between her fingers, she removed the satchel from the brooch that always held it in place along her waist. Slowly she opened the pouch and pulled the rune from it. Her fingers tingled at the sight of it, and she dropped the carved stone in her lap.

'Which way did he leave by?' Kenna asked, her voice a shaky tremble of air against her lips as she stood, the rune sliding from her lap to the rug.

Bridget stilled. She spied the carved token facing them. Recognising the slanted H symbol and what it meant, she paled.

'Which way?' Kenna cried out, desperate to know which way to run.

'West, towards the square,' Bridget finally answered, her voice quaking.

Kenna rushed from the room and slid on the rug on the hallway floor. She grabbed her cloak and shrugged it on. Yanking open the door, she skidded down the small set of icy stone stairs that led out to the cobblestone streets. Cold wind and sleet hit her face, and the merriment and music from the other homes and pubs nearby filled the air. Her chest tightened, her pulse increased and her long hair blew out behind her, the loose strands whipping along her cheeks.

He was fine. He was fine. The rune could be wrong.

But her runes were never wrong.

And she was never wrong about their meaning.

And that rune meant only one thing: *disruption.*

Something was wrong.

Kenna hurried down the streets, her gaze searching for her father and his tall, lanky frame that often stood out in such a crowd. Finally, she saw him. He was leaning against the side of a building, his face in profile, the features taut and strained. Relieved, she rushed to reach him, knocking into several passersby as she wove hastily through the revellers.

A man clutched her shoulder as she tried to pass. 'Stop,' he commanded. A flash of heat from the intensity of his hold on her arm sent a chill through Kenna's bones, and his fierce gaze stilled her, but she pulled free from him, desperate to see her father.

She faltered for a moment, as she thought the stranger had called out her name as she rushed on, but she ignored him. She didn't know him, so her mind had to be playing tricks on her. Soon she was swallowed up in the thickening crowd and the man was gone. No matter; she had no time for drunk men this eve. She had to reach her father.

'Father!' she called out, hoping she was close enough now for him to hear her over the din of the crowded streets.

He turned to her, his gaze resting on her in relief. He smiled and reached out a shaky hand to her. She grasped it and fell into him with a hug. He groaned and she froze.

'Father, where have you been? Bridget and I have been worried sick and...' She faltered at the feel of something warm and wet soaking into the front of her gown. Pulling back, she saw the blood on his chest and abdomen. She tugged his hand away from the wound. 'You are hurt!' She gasped. 'What happened? Who did this to you?'

He shushed her and squeezed her hands. 'My meeting with the stranger did not go as planned,' he said with a chuckle that made him cough. 'But I was right not to bring the parcel. It was not a Cameron that arrived to meet me.'

'What parcel? What meeting with the Cameron, Father? Who has done this to you?'

'I do not know, but he is gone now.'

She shouted for help, but the roar of revellers drowned out her cries.

'Shh…' her father said. 'There is no time. There is nothing to be done now but for you to listen.'

Her eyes filled with tears. 'I can go and get help. We can save you.'

'Nay.' He shook his head when she tried to utter another word. 'Listen. Listen to me.'

She bit her lip and clamped her mouth shut at the harshness in his voice, her gaze searching his soft sea-green eyes for answers and the familiar comfort they always brought her.

'There is a wrapped parcel hidden behind the inner workings of the old wall clock at home. You must deliver it to the Camerons at Loch's End in Argyll by the first of February. They *must* have it.'

'Why? What is so important about it?' she asked.

It all sounded delusional, odd and unlike anything Father had ever done before.

He shook his head. 'I have no time to explain. But you must take it to them yourself. It cannot be sent by courier or messenger. No one can be trusted now. And the MacDonalds...' He paused, coughing with effort. 'They must *not* discover you possess it. Ever.'

'Father, none of this makes sense. We do not know any Camerons or MacDonalds.'

'Aye.' He paused. 'But your mother does.'

Kenna stilled, her stomach turning in a sickening flip. 'My *mother* does? Is she alive?' she asked, desperate to know more. She had not seen her mother since she'd been ten years old. Dierdre Hay was presumed long dead, or perhaps that was merely what Kenna had been told.

'Aye,' he replied, dropping his gaze. 'She does. She is alive.'

'What? Why did you never tell me? We all presumed her dead after she left us.' Tears fell unbidden down her cheeks. Knowing her mother wilfully abandoned them *and* still lived was too hurtful to fathom.

'I know it is much to take in. I am sorry, my sweet. I wish I had more time...to explain. But you must take the parcel to your mother at the

Lost Village and then on to Loch's End yourself. No one else can deliver it but you. The Camerons will protect you until the threat from the MacDonalds is over. Then you can return to Melrose.' He squeezed her hands, his gaze a reflection of regret and uncertainty.

Confusion and doubt set in. 'I cannot do it, Father,' Kenna confessed. 'That is days from here, and I do not know the way.'

'You can and you must. The fate and future of the Highlands depends on it.'

'But…'

'You are strong,' he said with a smile. 'You are fearless and cunning. You are *my Enna*.'

Emotion filled her eyes at the sound of his nickname for her. 'I am none of those things, Father. Not without you.'

'Nay. You are all of those and more without me. You are a chameleon. Think of all the times you hid from me and I could not find you.' He squeezed her shoulders, and a tear fell down her cheek. 'Use that to make your way. And let the runes guide you. Listen to what they tell you. Trust yourself.'

'But I am no warrior, and I must cross the Borderlands to reach Argyll.'

'You do not have to be,' he replied, labouring to breathe. 'I have sent you a protector…and what you need to ease your way beyond that will come to you.'

'You always say that,' she murmured with a chuckle and a smile.

'I know.' He gasped. 'And I am always right. Let the runes guide you as they always have. You can and will do this. Promise me.' The desperation in his words and the draining light from his eyes cut her to the quick.

She hesitated and then swallowed hard, unwilling to let his last wish go unfulfilled, even if she didn't understand any of it and had no idea how to accomplish it. 'I promise,' she said with as much certainty as she could muster.

'That's my girl,' he murmured, relief softening his features. He pressed a kiss on her cheek before his eyes fluttered closed. Then he sagged forward in her arms and died.

Rolf Cameron gritted his teeth and clutched his hands into fists by his sides as he watched the poor young woman cradling her dying father in her arms. Standing in the shadows across the street, doing nothing to help her, tore against every part of who he was and made his skin itch. Walking away to let the old man bleed to death had been even harder, even if it had been a necessary evil.

The old man had commanded him to leave. 'Go—now. Danger is still near. The MacDonalds must believe I am dead. You must survive for her... for my daughter...and for your family. If you and my daughter do not succeed in gathering the parcel from the clock, and items from my wife Dierdre, all will be lost.'

All will be lost...

Rolf shuddered at all the possible meanings Bartholomew Hay's foreboding statement might have. Visions of loss and bloodshed flooded his mind again just as they had done in his dreams since the fateful day the first letter from Bartholomew Hay had arrived at Loch's End over a month ago.

Rolf ran a hand through his soaked hair, and the icy water sluiced down his neck and the ridges of his scarred back. It was a reminder of how he could fight to the end of his might if he needed to, which he just might need to do to protect this woman and gain the truth he sought. He rested his hand on the hilt of the blade tucked in the weapons belt that hid beneath his plaid and the heavy coat he wore over it.

He couldn't shake the feel of the young woman's strong shoulder in his hold and the haunted look in her sea-green eyes when he'd tried to stop her in the street minutes ago.

Bartholomew Hay's description of his daughter had been thorough and exact. 'She is tall, strong and lithe, like the sea winds, with long, auburn hair and eyes like mine. She has a power yet unleashed. You will feel it when you see her. You will know it is her. And you must, above all else, protect her. Promise me. She will help you save your clan and keep the MacDonalds at bay. She is the key to the secrets you seek, but she does not know it.'

Rolf sighed. His gut told him she was more than the key. She was trouble—trouble for him. He stretched his fingers off the hilt of his weapon and rolled his neck. The first sight and feel of her on the street had sent a jolt of longing in him he hadn't felt since... Joanna. Her vulnerability had ignited his innate need to protect, and even with the wind and sleet he'd been able to tell she was a beauty. Her dark auburn hair, gorgeous eyes, petite facial features and strong, lithe frame had lit a long-dormant flame of desire and want in him. Want for a life beyond the loneliness and solitude he clung to like the lifeline it was.

Even though his siblings had found their love matches and were planning lives full of family and happiness, Rolf knew no such future awaited him. He preferred being alone and focusing on his siblings and their growing families.

Liar.

In truth, he didn't believe he deserved such happiness and dared not risk loving again only to face loss right after it. And his fear of becoming anything resembling his parents, and living a life full of betrayal, secrets and shame, was enough to snuff out any desire for a family of his own.

But, the moment he'd touched Kenna Hay, she had looked straight through him in a way that had terrified him. As if she'd been able to see all those fears within him and the desires of his heart buried beneath them.

He bit his lip and frowned. Rolf had promised Bartholomew Hay that he would protect her in exchange for the secrets he needed answered, not bed her. That had been the bargain. He'd given his word to the old man before he'd died. And look at the wee lass: she'd never make it through the Borderlands, much less the trek through the Highlands in winter, without him. His chest tightened as he studied her once more.

Curses.

His fierce need to protect her flared into a raging fire in his gut. Rolf was in trouble.

He furrowed his brow. Or was he? Perhaps the woman was not the delicate flower he imagined. After all, Kenna Hay had shrugged him off with force when he'd tried to stop her earlier in the square. Her sole purpose had been to reach her father, who was now dead.

Rolf's jaw tightened. If he hadn't been delayed by the harsh weather on his journey from Loch's End to Melrose, he might have reached the poor man before he had been attacked and been able to do more than slow the blood escaping what they'd both known was a mortal wound. Now the old man and what he knew would be lost from this world, and Rolf had no answers and far more questions. What secrets had the man known that someone else would kill for?

There was only one way to find out. He had to keep his promise and be a guide and protector to Kenna Hay. Rolf had to know what this woman knew and what the old man had intended to give him. He watched the young woman clutching her father to her chest, trying to shield his body from the slushy sleet and rain that had just begun to fall again, and his chest tightened. He understood her grief. He'd lost both of his parents. He had grieved his mother deeply when he'd been younger and, although he had loved his father, he had struggled to feel anything but relief after his death. His cruelty had been so deep and the deceit that his family had discovered after his death about how the man had treated his children and his wife had made Rolf's blood cool.

While he knew he didn't have all the answers, he knew one thing for certain: his parents had had many secrets. Horrible secrets. And he was going to uncover them all, even if it was the last thing he'd do in this world. Keeping his siblings and their growing families safe mattered more to him than his own life or happiness. So he would watch Hay's daughter and work out how best to infiltrate himself into her life to get the answers he desired. While he didn't wish to be deceitful to get the information he needed, he would do what he had to, no matter how poorly he lied.

She is the key.

Hay's words echoed in Rolf's mind once more. He was a Cameron, after all. Family and clan loyalty would always be first in his heart. All else paled in comparison. He ran his finger over the good luck charm on the cord around his neck his sister Catriona had given him before he'd started out on this quest.

'Do not be a fool, brother,' she had whispered in his ear as she had clung tightly to him during their last embrace. 'Come back to us alive, whether you have discovered all or not. Your niece will need you.'

Rolf had smiled down at her. 'And what makes you so sure it is to be a girl?' he teased.

Catriona had pressed a hand to her full belly. 'I can see her beautiful cherub face when I close my eyes before I sleep. That is why.'

He'd clutched her hand, pushing down the emotion in his throat. She was such a survivor and having her back in their lives, after having believed her lost to the sea for over a decade, made him cherish their relationship even more, but he could not lie. It was one of his utter failings.

'You know I can promise no such thing.'

Her eyes had filled. 'I know,' she'd replied with emotion. 'You are honest beyond measure and I treasure it, brother.'

She'd pressed a hand to his chest, running her thumb over the smooth three-pence coin she had always kept in her shoe for protection. She had asked her new brother-in-law, Laird Rowan Campbell, to transform it into a pendant for Rolf as a Christmas gift for safety.

I hope this will bring you as much protection and comfort as it has always brought me.

The sound of Kenna Hay calling for help across the road yanked Rolf back from his memories. The odd coldness in her voice told him her father had died. Rolf clenched his fist by his side and continued to watch her, intrigued by how she shielded the dead man with her own body even after he had left this world. Her unwillingness to let him go even after others arrived to take him away moved Rolf, but he squared his shoulders and reminded himself that she was his mission, nothing more. He needed to protect her to gain the information he sought. Once he had that information, he would be on his way. His empathy for and instinctive attraction to her might well be his downfall if he wasn't careful.

And this mission was not one that could fail. The safety of his family and clan depended on his success. According to Bartholomew Hay, Kenna was the only one who could lead Rolf to the truth behind his father's secrets and finally grant the Camerons the peace and safety they craved. Without the truth, his family would be locked in a vice of uncertainty. They needed to know why the Mac-Donalds threatened their well-being, and why and, most importantly, how those secrets might endanger the Highlands and the next generation of Camerons on the way.

While Rolf was willing to accept the consequences of his parents' actions, he wasn't willing to have his future nieces and nephews endure the same. The innocents deserved better, and part of him knew he and his siblings did too.

Chapter Two

North of Melrose,
a week later

Kenna rested on her back on the cold, frozen ground and stared up at the dark, cloudy sky. Sleep would not come no matter how hard she willed it or how tired she felt. It had been a week since her father's passing and only one day since his burial. Her chest tightened. She missed him. She missed everything about him. Her eyes burned as the cold air hit the moisture of the tears that threatened. She was alone, so very alone in this world now, save Bridget. Kenna didn't like it one bit. In fact, she was enraged by it.

How dared someone kill her father? And for

what—to keep a secret? For the decaying letters and solitary map she'd found wrapped like a parcel in the inner workings of her father's old wall clock? All for clans she did not know or care about. And how dare her father make her promise to fulfil this ridiculous quest? She didn't know any Camerons or MacDonalds and, since they had caused her father's death, she had no wish to.

None of what had happened since the night of Hogmanay made sense, and she had tried to puzzle it out for days and nights with no success. She linked her hands together and rested them on her stomach under the wool blanket covering her. What did one do without a father? Was it just like not having a mother? She knew what that felt like.

She frowned. Well, at least she *had*. Now, she evidently had a mother after all, in this 'Lost Village' denoted on the map she'd found on top of the bound letters. So, her mother had abandoned her and not died. The fresh betrayal of her parents' lies and her father's sudden death made her question everything.

Had anyone in this world other than Bridget ever told her the absolute truth? Her poor housemaid had been equally surprised to hear that Kenna's mother was alive. Bridget's tears of betrayal and shock had matched Kenna's own, and together they had weathered the grief of the last few days. Leaving Bridget to fulfil this promise to her father had been painful, but Kenna needed it to be the one good thing to come out of the chaos and sadness of his death.

Deep down, Kenna didn't believe any good could come out of his death, but she'd set out anyway. A promise was a promise. She had consulted the runes and they had been in her favour, beckoning her on, and they were never, ever wrong. She rested her hand on the pouch that hung at her weapons belt. They were as much a weapon to her as the rather dull dagger she had found in her father's store.

The large field and cove to the right would be enveloped in frost and frozen mist come daybreak, judging by the dropping temperatures. Soon, Kenna's teeth would be chattering. Even now, she watched the spirals of warm air escape her lips like smoke from a chimney and twine up into the sky until they disappeared into nothingness, much like she hoped she would once morning came. While her ridiculous soldier disguise had passed muster when she'd joined the ranks of men under the cover of darkness this eve, she wasn't so sure about how she would be greeted in the daylight. Kenna winced and tugged on the tight cloth strips Bridget had used to bind her breasts. Kenna had a rather demure bosom as it was. Wrapped, she was almost flat. Why had she agreed to this ridiculous disguise?

She sighed and snuggled deeper into the single wool blanket she had brought with her until only her eyes were exposed to the chill. She knew exactly why she had agreed to Bridget's ridiculous suggestion of a disguise as a Jacobite soldier: because there was no other way Kenna could fulfil her promise to her father. How else could she safely travel through the Borderlands to find her mother at this Lost Village without help?

While she knew the general direction based on the map, she still found the drawings confusing. Joining the ranks of the Jacobite army as it passed through seemed the best option. Her father's promise of a 'protector' arriving for her had yet to materialise, and the runes had made no mention of one arriving soon. She pulled up her large trews so they rested a bit higher on her hips and settled into the discordant snores surrounding her.

This had become her life. Strangely, it hadn't been as hard as she had expected to slip in amongst the ranks of soldiers earlier that eve. Being covered up for the weather, with her hair hidden under a wool cap and wearing her father's clothes, she believed she looked more pathetic than dangerous. She was thin by nature, but the large clothes made her look as if she were a half-starved young lad.

The first soldier who had laid eyes upon her had offered her some dried beef. To decline would have seemed rude, so she'd grunted in thanks, nodded and yanked off a bit of it with her teeth. She'd forced herself to swallow it despite it tasting like burnt leather. She had scarcely stifled a gag before she'd fallen in step amongst them as they had begun the climb to where they were now, wherever that was. It seemed to be the middle of nowhere. She swallowed hard. If she disappeared, no one would even know. Well, at least Bridget would suspect what had happened. She was the only one who knew where she was heading to and perhaps the only one who even cared.

Curses.

Kenna blinked back tears. She was turning into a wallowing mess, feeling sorry for herself lying amongst a sea of hardened soldiers. If she was to fulfil this promise to her father to reach Loch's End in Argyll, the stronghold of the Cameron clan, she needed to set aside her sadness over her situation, toughen up and focus on the present. She sniffed and frowned when she smelled something: *smoke.* She scanned the night sky above her and didn't see anything except for clouds, but there was smoke somewhere. Shifting on the ground, she looked to the right and then left.

Smoke billowed from the woods. She froze. She could hear it now, the soft crackling of tree limbs burning, the slow creaking of fire in the forest they slept close to. She rolled onto her stomach, keeping the blanket over her nose and mouth. Could it have happened naturally? She studied the spurts of light coming from within the trees.

Doubtful. The fire was fierce and moving fast. Besides, soldiers such as these would never have dared have a fire so close to the brush, let alone leave it to burn unattended when so many men camped and slept nearby. They had made camp between villages, from what she could tell of the area around them, and had few places to hide other than the cove that sat opposite the forest. The only option that remained was to retreat to the cove, but if this was a trap the enemy would await them there.

The smoke thickened and the crackling of the fire intensified behind her in the woods. Was that the heat of the flames warming her or fear flushing her body? Did it matter? She rose to her elbows and squinted out into the darkness. Why was no one else awake? And how did she dare sound an alarm to warn the men without drawing undue attention to herself or getting killed?

She doubted soldiers would respond well to a shout to wake.

Blast.

She slithered across the grass to the men who slept closest to her. 'Fire,' she whispered. They did not move. She clutched the shoulder of a young soldier and shook it. 'Fire,' she said a bit louder. His eyes flashed open. Then he flipped her onto her back and pinned her with his weight. He slammed her wrist to the ground and clutched her by the throat, as if he were under attack. She coughed. 'Fire,' she sputtered again weakly, gasping for air. She glanced behind her.

He followed her gaze, scanned the woods and then glanced back down at her. His eyes widened and he released her, no doubt realising she was not the enemy after all. He cursed, stood and shouted. 'Fire!' he warned, bellowing loud and clear to the men who slept around them. She reached for one of his boots and coughed, trying to warn him of the danger she sensed surrounding them.

The distinctive crisp swish of an arrow sliced through the air before hitting him square in the chest. He landed hard next to her, his eyes wide and lifeless. Gasping, she swallowed a scream and clambered backwards. Her eyes watered. She'd been too late in warning him. He was dead.

As other men woke in the confusion, Kenna sat stunned, unable to take her eyes from the dead man she had awakened moments before.

Had she killed him?

'Fire!' more men shouted to one another, and the flames grew from the woods. The added light aided her in seeing dark shadows off in the distance near the cove. They started moving. They were under attack.

'They're coming,' she said softly and then her voice gained strength. She shouted it this time. 'They're coming, from the cove!'

The enemy picked up pace, now running with purpose. The outline of their drawn bows could not be mistaken, nor the large blades and swords they clutched in their hands as they crested the hill. The sickening sound of sluicing arrows cut the air once more. The arrows hit their targets around her, and the groans of wounded men followed.

She stifled a scream and scrambled to her knees. She was about to push up to stand and run when a hand clamped over her mouth and another cinched her waist, causing her to fold her body over. She was being dragged backwards, closer to the heat of the flames. She tried to cry out, but the hand clamped over her mouth and the shouts of the other men drowned her out. She kicked and flailed, but the man was too strong, so strong that her boot heels dragged against the ground despite how hard she tried to slow his progress.

The enemy had her. How had he even reached her from the cove? And why had the man not just killed her? Was he planning to interfere with her? Did he somehow know from her screams that she was a woman and not a man? She had to escape him. She elbowed the man hard in the gut and he grunted.

'Stop,' he snapped near her ear. 'Stop fighting me,' he commanded, his voice harsh and unyielding with a tinge of impatience, as if she were a petulant child. 'I am *not* your enemy,' he added.

Yield. The word came to her in her father's voice. She ignored it and kicked against the man's shins, hard.

'Cease,' he said loudly. 'Your father sent me,' he added, whispering near her ear as she landed another blow to his thigh.

'He is dead,' she mumbled against the hand covering her mouth. She opened her mouth to bite it, but he pulled his hand away quickly.

'I know, Miss Hay. He sent me before he died to protect you.'

Father.

He said a protector would come.

Yield.

It echoed again in her mind. Despite every instinct to continue to fight, Kenna ceased and her arms dropped listlessly to her sides.

The man stilled and cupped her chin before roughly turning her face to him. He scanned her features and body. 'Are you hurt?' he asked, his brow furrowed and the lines around his mouth tight.

'Nay,' she replied, studying him. 'I am tired.'

Of everything.

There was something about his face, his eyes and the intensity of his hold that was familiar. Gooseflesh rose along her skin. 'Wait. I know you,' she whispered, still not able to place where she knew this man from.

'Aye. And I know you, Kenna Hay. We must go—now.' He clutched her hand in his own and ran, half-dragging her behind him.

'Keep up,' he commanded as they cut through the battling soldiers, but her legs felt soft and weak, much like when she'd been a child recovering from fever. She lagged, no matter how hard she tried to focus on putting one foot in front of the other. A flash of the face of the man who had been killed right before her after she had awakened him made her stomach turn. She fell to her knees and retched.

The flames of the forest sent a chill through her body as the heat hit the sweat on the back of her neck and arms. She retched again.

The man cursed but waited until she'd finished.

She wiped her mouth, but dizziness overcame her. She could hear the shouts and screams of men dying in the distance and the sound of clanging weaponry. 'We should help them,' she muttered.

'Nay,' he argued. 'Your death will serve no one, nor would mine. And you have a greater purpose, Miss Hay.' Before she could ask him how he knew this, or her, he hefted her entire body over his shoulder as if she were a sack of grain. Her face smacked into his back, which was as solid as a tree trunk.

'Ow!' she complained, and crinkled her nose, which had taken the brunt of the impact.

'Apologies, miss. We are out of options. Hold on.'

She blinked up at the side of his face, which was all she could see. His profile and features were still familiar, but she could not place him.

Drat. She cursed her muddled mind.

'Use my plaid to cover your nose and mouth

from the smoke,' he offered, and then slid a portion of the tartan up and over his nose and mouth.

Wait. Did he mean to run through the woodlands—the burning woodlands?

Before she could utter a word, he charged into the flaming forest. She gasped, clutched the loose gathering of plaid covering his back, and covered her mouth and nose with it. With the other arm, she clung to his torso to prevent her head from being smacked against his tree trunk of a back again. With every movement, muscles rippled beneath his skin, and she squeezed her eyes shut to keep her churning stomach at bay.

Yield.

Father's voice echoed through her again, and she softened her hold so her body could move along with the man's own movements rather than stiffly against him. It was as if she were riding a horse.

Nay, it was nothing of the sort, but it reduced the strain and ache in her arms. The heat surrounding her intensified and sweat beaded her skin and dampened the man's plaid as she held it. He slowed, moving with skill and purpose rather than speed, his breaths ragged and harsher now. The sounds of death and battle disappeared and only the sound of him and the cracking of burning trees and their limbs as they fell to the ground remained.

Suddenly, he stopped. Something was wrong. She coughed and dared to open her eyes. Cloudy smoke and fire surrounded them. Her eyes watered and burned.

'Left,' she cried out. She didn't know why, but the direction had sprung to her mind clearly and unbidden, a stark contrast to the muddled mind she'd had before.

The man paused.

'Left,' she said again with certainty, as if she were commanding his movements. He cursed and then veered left, hissing as a rogue flame singed through his plaid and burned his forearm. She winced and squeezed her eyes shut. Why was he doing this? And how did he know who she was? And why could she not remember where she had met him?

He hissed again and she cringed. Why had she said 'left'? The man was getting wounded… because of her. Just like the man she had woken who'd died trying to warn the others of the attack. The image of her father dying claimed her mind. Had she been the cause of that too? *Curses.* She was being ridiculous. She hadn't caused her father's death.

She stiffened. Her father's death: that was how she remembered this strange man. He had clutched her shoulder as she had been desperate to reach her father in the street. He had tried to stop her, but why? And he'd known her name. He'd known her. He had called her by name, her name: *Miss Hay.*

He had called her by her name without hesitation.

You have a greater purpose, Miss Hay.

She shivered. Exactly what kind of purpose? She read runes, she could solve puzzles, she could improvise and she could tell an antique from an imitation. What kinds of skills were those to anyone other than her father? What greater purpose could she as the daughter of an antique dealer possibly have?

Her heart picked up speed and thundered in her chest. A chill overcame her despite the intense heat of the burning woods they ran through. He had been there that night on the street—she was sure of it—and he was here now. How had he even found her? Had he been following her or stalking her? Had her father really sent him? Or was he kidnapping her for some purpose beyond her imaginings?

Dread crept along her skin. She could try to flee…but she would stand little chance of surviving. The man was strong, skilled and intelligent. Otherwise, they would already be dead. She had to allow him to take her from the burning woods before she tried to escape him. Or perhaps she could wait until he was asleep. Then she might have a sliver of a chance of escaping.

Kenna kept her head down as they continued through the forest. The heat had subsided and now merely felt warm, and the bright light from the flames had softened into a glow. In the distance there appeared to be an opening and an end to the burning woodlands, but what was beyond that she didn't know. She no longer had any idea where she was, and it was so dark she couldn't spot any landmarks.

After a few more minutes, they emerged from the woods into an open field. It was dark and quiet. The man who had been carrying her collapsed to his knees and placed her gently on the ground. He scanned her face and body. His features relaxed when he found her unharmed, and he panted for breath, coughing. She bit her lip. Now was the perfect time to flee. He wouldn't expect it. She began to stand. He reached out quickly and clamped a hand around her wrist.

'Do…not…run,' he ground out, staring at her.

She froze in his hold, and his gaze locked with hers.

'Why not?' she countered softly. 'You have kidnapped me.' She paused before continuing. 'I do not know you. You said my father sent you, but how do I know you have not killed him yourself? I remember you from the street. You clutched my arm. You tried to stop me from reaching him and saving him that day.'

He released her wrist. He scoffed and gulped in a few more breaths before sitting back on his haunches and resting his hands on his knees. His face was darkened with soot and sweat, and his hair was damp and hung long around his face.

'Is that what you believe?' he asked, and shook his head. He brushed his hair back from his face, revealing strong, angular features. 'You are a fool—not the clever woman your father described. Why would I save your life by dragging you from a fiery battlefield if I planned to kill you or hurt you? And why would I stab your father and remain in the streets watching?'

He stood and wiped his face with a portion of his plaid, and she saw the burns along his arms where his plaid had been charred through.

He had a few points, but she was reluctant to accept any of them. 'Explain it to me, then, so I *do* understand,' she replied, crossing her arms against her chest. The weight of her bag of runes against her thigh was a familiar comfort.

'I am fulfilling an agreement I made with your father.'

'An agreement?' She balked.

'Aye. A contract of sorts. He has paid me to be your guide. I promised him that I would protect you along your journey…so you could deliver your message north to the Camerons.' His gaze dropped away from her.

'Are you my protector?' she whispered, her stomach dropping to her feet like a rock at the confirmation of what she had thought earlier.

'Aye.' The word rang with resignation and fatigue. 'But I find you to be a hard woman to protect.'

Chapter Three

This interrogation of hers was like a slow death. The hidden truths Rolf held back were like tiny barbs on his tongue. He hated lying, but it seemed necessary. Miss Hay was a handful and would not be persuaded easily.

He studied his charge. She was covered in grime from the fire and her disguise as a soldier with her father's large trews, tunic, plaid and overcoat hung off her slight frame as if she were a bird scarer set in a field to guard crops. Her large eyes were wide and pleading, desperate to understand him, it seemed, and what he had just done to her, which in all good sense *had* been kidnapping. The thick coiled braid pinned to her head like a crown beneath the hat she had been wearing had loosened in their rush to escape, and long, loose tendrils of her auburn hair framed her face and drifted past her shoulders.

Despite it all, she entranced him. In a word, she was beautiful.

He was in deep trouble.

She stared at him for a long minute before edging closer to him. 'Are *you* my protector?' she asked again. 'Will you guide me to my mother and then to the Highlands to deliver Father's parcel to the Camerons?'

'Aye,' he answered, swallowing back the uncertainty as he held her gaze. It wasn't a lie, exactly, but it felt like one. His pulse increased as she came even closer. Her intimate assessment of him unsettled him, as if she could see through him. Gooseflesh rose along his skin as he was able to take in the subtle sea-green of her eyes and smears of dirt and smoke upon her cheeks.

'Why?' she asked, a single, simple word that had no simple answer.

Liar.

There was a simple answer, but he was loath to share it. 'As I said before, he paid me. Well…' He dug in the pouch secured to his weapons belt. 'He gave me this,' he offered, showing her what Bartholomew Hay had handed him before he'd passed.

'To reach the Lost Village…and your mother. It is a hand-drawn map.'

She looked at it. 'Aye. It is like the one he gave me, but this is a version in smaller scale.'

He tensed, preparing himself for her rebuke at his half-truths. To his surprise, she nodded, considering his explanation and the map further. He relaxed.

'And when you grabbed my arm in the street—what were you doing there?'

He gritted his teeth. He should have expected the question. The woman was no fool. In truth, her stubborn determination reminded him of his sister Susanna.

'I did not kill him, as you accused me of, if that is your next enquiry,' he countered, feeling as irritated as he oft did under Susanna's barrage of questions. He was tired and frustrated and lying took too much energy—energy he no longer had.

He scanned his surroundings and spied a small outcropping that could provide them some shelter from the wind at least. 'Follow me. You can continue your questioning of me and my intentions out of the elements. We are too exposed here.'

He started off towards the rock outcropping, but she didn't immediately fall in step behind him. He mumbled in frustration but kept going. She would follow him, as the woman had good sense, but he couldn't force her to. She would do so when she was ready. It was becoming quite apparent that their journey together would be a long one. But he had to get Miss Hay to the village where her mother was. The older woman was the next key to whatever piece of the puzzle Rolf sought, or at least he hoped so.

There was a small part of him that feared the whole decision to come here might have been a mistake, and that he had fallen for a ruse to leave the clan and his family further exposed. It had been less than a fortnight, but he missed them all desperately, even his new brother-in-law, Rowan. Rolf had taken on the charge of learning some of the fundamental skills of the blacksmith from his brother-in-law, as he saw how it calmed his mind and restlessness.

How Rolf needed it now. He had found that the more settled and content his siblings became as they started their own families, the more untethered, lost and restless he felt. For who was he without his family? Who was he at all?

Focus.

He needed to be alert. Danger could be anywhere.

He approached the outcropping slowly, anticipating that it might have already been claimed by another man or animal. He took deep breaths, in the hope of smelling any other creatures that might be there, but only encountered the familiar odour of damp soil and the remnants of smoke still in his nostrils. He ran his fingers along the layer of rock that jutted out above him. It was free of debris, and insects as well, so he felt confident that it would provide them with a good night of sleep and rest.

Or at least it would, if he had something else to keep them warm. All he had was the stolen tartan wrapped over his tunic and trews and the singed coat he wore over it. Miss Hay had a tartan and coat as well, but both had lost their wool blankets in the rush to escape the fire. It would be a cold night. So far, he seemed to be failing at his job as protector. The woman had almost been killed by fire and flying arrows, and now she might well freeze to death.

He heard her soft approach in the grass behind him and turned. 'We will take shelter here until morn,' he said. 'Then, we will work out where we are and how we shall reach the village.'

She remained standing at the threshold of the outcropping, unwilling to advance. 'Who are you?' she asked.

'Rolf,' he replied simply, unwilling to share his full identity with her.

'And how did my father meet you?' she asked, staring at him.

'His work.'

'And you were on the streets that night because…?'

'I was supposed to pick up something from him,' he replied.

Her eyes widened. 'Supposed to?' she asked. 'Did you not get it?'

'Nay. He had already been wounded.'

She balked. 'And you left him alone to die in the street?'

He pulled back his shoulders and frowned at her accusation. 'I left him to reach you, as he'd ordered me to. He was worried for your safety, and he had good reason to be.'

'Why?' she asked, coming closer. 'What do you know about who attacked him?'

'Nothing, except they were skilled with a blade. He died quickly,' he countered, taking a step towards her, angry over her incessant questions and accusations.

She sucked in a breath and hurt registered in her gaze.

Curses. He hadn't meant to be cruel, but he

needed to stop this line of questioning before he said too much or gave himself away. Her curiosity was a threat to her safety, but she didn't know that. The less she knew, the safer she would be. Her father had died trying to help him uncover the secrets of his family's past. The idea of her suffering the same fate angered him. He simply wouldn't let it happen, whether she hated him or not.

'Could it have been one of the Camerons he was supposed to meet that killed him?'

'Nay,' he said, swallowing through the lie that tightened his throat. 'They wouldn't want him dead if they needed information from him.' Her pointed enquiries and his half-true answers made his feet itch, but what choice did he have? The woman didn't trust him, and he needed her to.

'Or the MacDonalds?' she asked. 'Were they so desperate to get the information he had that they killed him?'

'That might be more plausible, but I would think they would want the information too. I believe it was an outsider.'

'But you don't know that for certain,' she argued.

'Nay, I don't,' he agreed. 'We may never know what happened to him.'

'Well, I hate the Camerons and the MacDonalds,

and I will tell them so when I meet them in Loch's End to deliver this ridiculous parcel to them. They have ruined my life,' she finished, angry unshed tears brightening her eyes in the darkness of the cave.

His gut twisted in agony—her agony and the agony he knew paired so well with grief. He swallowed hard and fought the instinct to pull her into his arms and console her.

Distance would keep his mind clear; her touch wouldn't. He was beginning to care for her and her feelings too much already.

'Sleep here,' he commanded.

'Is that the end of our discussion?' she asked, emotion raising the pitch of her voice.

'For now. Rest; I will keep watch.'

'All night?' she said.

'Aye.'

'And fall over from fatigue?' She scoffed. She shook her head, shrugged off her coat and placed it neatly on the ground. 'I will sleep first, then you will wake me after a few hours, and then I will stand watch.'

He chuckled. 'You will stand watch?'

She lifted her brow in challenge. 'Aye. I may be a woman, but I am more than capable of watching for danger.'

He had no idea what to make of this slip of a woman. She was fragile, yet strong; interesting and yet grating; challenging and yet exhilarating all at the same time.

Curses. He was in far more trouble than he'd first thought. Then, he reminded himself of Joanna, and the flash of lust in him disintegrated into dust. Even though it had been years ago, her brutal rejection of him for being merely the second son, after he had asked her to marry him, could not be borne again. He had scarcely recovered and had kept his interest in women strictly to his bed. Stomping out his attraction to this woman early on would benefit them both, no matter how his pulse quickened at the sight of her. All he needed was his family. They were all that mattered now.

'You will wake me in four hours. Promise me,' she commanded.

He crossed his arms against his chest. He had no intention of promising to do anything of the sort. He was *her* protector, not the other way around.

'Fine,' she grumbled, lying down and snuggling as best she could into the coat and tartan she had to cover herself as she slept. 'I will wake myself.'

He scoffed and shook his head. Wake herself? Ridiculous.

She mumbled something he couldn't quite decipher before she closed her eyes.

'You never told me your surname, *Rolf*,' she said with obvious disdain.

I hate the Camerons and the MacDonalds... They have ruined my life.

He paused as he remembered her words from moments before. Glancing down at the dark-green-and-red tartan he had stolen from another soldier to ease into the ranks unnoticed, a seed of an idea formed. He'd known his Cameron plaid would be spotted and identified easily due to their wealth and power and had grabbed the Dunbar tartan on instinct to blend into the ranks. Perhaps the plaid would serve a finer purpose now in disguising his identity from her.

He paused and uttered his first big lie to her. 'Dunbar,' he offered. 'My name is Rolf Dunbar.'

'Hmmm,' she murmured, studying his tartan. 'I have never known any Dunbars.'

'We are a smaller clan just east of Inverness. There is no reason you would have,' he added, his throat drying from the shock of the lies as they continued to flow so easily from his lips. His heart pounded and he opened and closed his fist by his side. He'd had no choice but to lie to her, had he? She would have fled if he had told her the truth.

She hated the Camerons and the MacDonalds; she had said so herself. In her eyes, he and his family had killed her father.

His chest tightened. Maybe, in a way, they had. Bartholomew Hay had died protecting the secrets of his family and the Highlands. But why? What connection did the man have to Rolf's family or to the MacDonalds that he would take such a risk, especially with his daughter? Why had the future of the Highlands mattered to him at all?

All the questions and the physical and emotional strain of the day leeched out what remained of Rolf's mental energy.

Just focus on her, he commanded himself.

Keeping her alive and getting her to the Lost Village were his next steps. After they reached the village safely, he would forge the next portion of his plan to get back to Loch's End with whatever information they uncovered. He would do his best to dissuade her from pursuing the last leg of their journey. There was no need for her to travel all that way, no matter what Bartholomew Hay had made her promise.

Rolf watched Kenna Hay until the gentle rhythmic rise and fall of her chest denoted sleep, and his shoulders finally relaxed. What a hellish day it had been. Although she didn't know how close to death she had come, he did. If he'd taken a second longer to grab her, an arrow would have hit her square in the chest. His breath hitched. This simple promise to Bartholomew Hay to protect his daughter and get her to her mother would be a difficult one to fulfil. And who knew how long it would then take to secure his mother's letters and the truth behind Bartholomew Hay's secrets to help Rolf unravel his own?

He struggled to understand what his parents had done in the past and why. Just thinking but a moment upon how his father had left his sister Catriona on the isle of Lismore when he'd discovered she was there after having been lost at sea still astounded him. Knowing she'd been fathered by Laird MacDonald rather than his own father was even harder to fathom. His parents' deceit had woven a complicated web of tragedy and confusion around him and his siblings, and Rolf desperately wanted to be free of it before any nieces or nephews were born—but how? The truth seemed desperate to remain hidden. But he was even more determined to uncover it. He hoped the cost of achieving such a goal would not be too great.

His gaze drifted back to Kenna Hay. The woman was an innocent bystander, and had no real involvement in his scheme with her father, yet here she was risking her life to help fulfil a promise to her father she didn't understand. He stilled. Was he doing the same? He shifted on his feet, uncomfortable with the idea despite how true it might be. He was desperate for a new start for his siblings and for a different and bright future for them all.

She slept soundly, despite what they had been through. Even the soot from the smoke could not mask her beauty. Nor could the too-large clothes hanging off her tall, lithe frame. He swallowed hard. Kenna Hay was the key to unlocking the truth he desired, and he would protect her with his life. He just hoped he didn't lose himself in the process.

Kenna squinted at the early-dawn light as it hit her face. The man had not woken her. She cursed and sat up quickly, too quickly. She groaned at the ache in her body. She ached everywhere, and in places she hadn't even known she possessed muscles. She fought the urge to lie back down, despite how stiff and numb her backside felt after a night of sleep on the frozen ground.

'Good morn,' Rolf called to her as he crouched down to walk into the covered outcropping. Her eyes widened as she took in his full presence. He was tall, even taller than her father, and his frame was thick but muscular. His tunic pulled against his shoulders and forearms, and she could see wounded flesh through the thin fabric of the tunic that had been lanced and burned through by the fire the night before. His hair was dark with a hint of a wave and touched the base of his neck. He had strong, sharp features and looked more like a Viking god than a man.

She blinked at him. Had he been this tall and this large yesterday? Had he been this ungodly handsome? She studied him in silence. *Was this even the same man?*

He cocked his head to the side as he scanned her face. 'Are you unwell?' he asked. 'You look a bit…' he gestured to her face and paused '…ill.'

It was then she realised she was staring, blatantly staring. A bit of a flush heated her cheeks, and she pulled up her jacket collar to her chin. A rush of the events of the night before clicked through her mind and she stilled. This man had carried her through a raging forest fire on his back like a sack of grain. Humiliation registered alongside her confusion.

Then, she was consumed by a wave of uncertainty and distrust. She was here with this man, a strange man, who claimed to be her protector to get her to the Lost Village, but what did she really know about him? She needed more proof than his word. 'Who are you again?' she asked.

'Rolf Dunbar. Same as what I told you yesterday, Miss Hay,' he said. His annoyance was not well hidden. He brought himself back to his full height as he entered the larger space within the cave and rested his hands on his waist-belt. 'It is dawn. We need to get moving while we have the light,' he urged. 'If you need to…' he said, gesturing to the woods off in the distance '…before we depart, there is a safe area at the edge of the tree-line that I already scouted out.'

She sat up as straight as she could and pulled back her shoulders. 'And why should I believe you are who you say and that you will take me where I need to go? How do I know you are truly the protector my father spoke of?'

He sighed, as if she were a sullen child. 'What proof do you require?' He scowled, crossing his arms against his chest, which just made him look more Viking-like and foreboding.

'The map. I want to see the map Father supposedly gave you more closely.'

'There is no "supposedly". He gave me a map.' He pulled it from his waist-belt but didn't hand it to her. He lifted a brow and quirked his lip. 'And I would like to see what you have.'

'What I have where?' she asked, flushing and uncertain of his meaning.

'What your father gave you about the Lost Village and this search, Miss Hay. Surely, it will help aid our journey?'

Kenna bit her lip. She wasn't so sure if what her father left her in the wrapped parcel in the old wall clock would help them at all. When she'd opened it, she'd discovered a map, a collection of letters, and a bound diary with runic symbols and notes that even she could not decipher. Perhaps she would only show him the letters and maps for now. It was too soon to try to explain her gift as a rune caster to the man; one never knew how a person would react to such news. Some men were believers while others viewed her gifts to be sinister or akin to witchcraft. She knew they were neither, but merely guidance from the universe. Guidance that she was very keen and eager to receive, as it was never wrong.

'Well?' he asked.

'I have a map and letters,' she rushed out.

His scowl fell away, and he came to her, offering his hand to help her to stand. Tentatively, she accepted it. The warmth and strength of his hold enveloped her even though he was only clutching her hand. He pulled her to her feet with ease. A rush of awareness seized her when she realised she was still holding his hand. She pressed her lips together and released a breath as she let go.

She dug in the large pocket Bridget had sewn into one of her father's old coats where she had stored the items. Slowly she removed the letters and map, careful not to reveal the bound diary nestled there. 'They appear to be from a single person, as the writing is quite distinctive,' she offered, extending the bundle of bound letters towards him.

He hesitated, staring at them. 'Have you read them?' he asked quietly.

'Only some. I could not decipher how they would help us at all. They appear to be love letters.'

'Love letters?' He looked stricken, as if this was the worst possible news she could have shared.

She shrugged. 'I do not understand why my father hid them either. Perhaps they will mean something to my mother.'

He shook his head, not wanting to take the letters from her. 'No bother, then. Complete your ablutions and return. We will set out at once.'

She tucked the map and letters back into their pocket, nodded, and left for the woods, confused by his sudden change of mood. Was he merely upset that she had only letters and a map to aid their journey or was it something else? He had been excited at seeing the letters until she'd told him they were love letters. It was then he'd turned cold—squeamish, even. Was the idea of reading a man and woman's devotion to one another so appalling?

Just when she'd thought she was beginning to understand this Rolf Dunbar a wee bit, he'd gone odd on her. Her runes pressed their weight along her thigh, a sign that she should indeed consult them. She glanced back to find the man watching her keenly; his scowl had returned. While she might be a difficult woman to protect, he would be a difficult man to be protected by. Their journey together would be long, it seemed, if the last half day was any indication, especially with him so reluctant to share anything about himself.

Just as she was. They would be a pair, would they not?

She shook her head, found a safe but secluded spot in the woods and completed her ablutions. Finally, she removed the binding that secured her breasts in a brutal hold. The relief was immediate, and she sighed.

After getting dressed, she soaked in her surroundings. Despite the chaos of the night before, she couldn't ignore the fierce winter beauty of the morn now. The frozen grass crunched lightly beneath her feet as she walked, the ice glimmering in the soft, golden glow of the dawn. The sunrise was transforming the sky into colourful layered waves of oranges and pinks, as if they were twining out from the treetops. The forest from where they had escaped the night before still smoked, but the distance between it and them was impressive.

Had Mr Dunbar truly carried her that far on his own in the dead of night? She shivered. While the morn was quiet and no battles raged, the echoes of the night before were not too far back in her memory. She shivered as she reached the cove where her protector awaited her.

'Do you believe anyone else survived?' Kenna asked, thinking upon whether others like them might have been lucky enough to escape.

He shrugged and scanned the woods and valleys off in the distance from where they had come. 'Perhaps,' he said. 'But unlikely. Being attacked at night by surprise doesn't often lead to many survivors.'

'How did you even know I was there?' she asked, wondering for the first time just how he had been in the right place at the right time.

'I had been following you.'

'Then why not reveal yourself at my father's funeral? Or the handful of days between his murder and my joining the group of soldiers?'

He shrugged and looked away. 'I did not know if you would even follow through with your promise to him. If you had not, I would not have been needed as your protector. I cannot fulfil his promise if you don't.'

She frowned. 'So, you fulfilling your promise to my father was dependent on what I did? That seems odd.'

'Aye. Our duties to him are intertwined. We cannot achieve them alone.' He removed the map from his waist-belt and began studying the horizon and the hillsides stretching out to their north and west.

The man was hiding something from her again, she could feel it, but what?

He met her scrutinising gaze. 'What?' he asked.

'I do not believe you have told me the whole truth, *protector*,' she accused, emphasizing his duty to protect her despite the fact she failed to trust him.

'Then that makes two of us, Miss Hay,' he replied. 'But we are stuck together until we complete this mission to reach the Camerons, are we not? Come. We must reach the top of that ridge before nightfall. Snow is coming.'

Chapter Four

Saints be.

The woman was more vexing than any he'd ever met, which Rolf hadn't thought possible. Kenna was also as sharp as both his sisters, which brought along its own complications. He frowned. It would be challenging to continue this charade of vagueness and deception for much longer with Miss Hay, but he had to continue to try. She would be less than forthcoming once she learned he was a Cameron and likely partly to blame for what had happened to her father.

He wouldn't even blame her for her anger. He understood; he would have felt the same. Part of him felt sorry for her.

He picked up the cadence of his strides as he

climbed the frozen pathway through the valley. He couldn't afford to feel anything for her. He stamped down any concern he had for her besides using her for what she knew and who she knew.

Deep down, he knew this was a ridiculous expectation. Father had always chided him for his softness.

Feelings are a nuisance best discarded! His father would exclaim that before slapping Rolf on the side of the face. Even now the memory of the sting of the force of it could make his eyes water. He pressed his tongue to the side of his cheek. The body had a memory unlike the mind, but equally fierce. And a father's cruelty was hard to forget. It trapped boys inside of men, as it had Rolf.

There were days when he felt like the small eight-year-old boy who'd lost his mother and been commanded by his father not to cry. On other days, he felt like the man he was—or at least the one he longed to be every day.

On yet other days, he wasn't sure who he was at all. He felt like a stranger carrying around a huge, invisible bag on his shoulders, lugging it behind him without any hope of discarding the extra weight and unable to find a place to unburden himself. He couldn't even tell his family how he felt. They would claim it was just how he was, and whatever other useless platitude they could think of to brush off the discomfort of feeling too much.

His heart picked up speed; he sucked in a breath through his teeth and held it, trying to slow the churning that had begun inside his body. He let go of the breath and took another. Soon, his heart slowed back down. Aye, he was trapped, but maybe, just maybe, uncovering the secrets of his past and his childhood would set him free.

Free from himself.

Free from the past.

Free to live…a life.

A life of his own without fear and regret.

A life of his own without the expectations of family.

The idea of it intrigued him as much as it terrified him. What was he besides the youngest brother—the peacemaker? Or the frightened boy who'd been always watchful and waiting for the next rebuke from his father? He didn't know, but part of him longed to find out. He had lost himself long ago, but with each passing day he felt more and more desperate to get that part of himself back and to see what life might hold for him without such fears and regrets.

'Where are we going?' Miss Hay called from behind him.

Her question yanked him back to the present and the mission at hand. 'To the Lost Village.' Or at least where the blasted place was supposed to be.

'Have you been there before?' she asked. 'It sounds rather…foreboding.' Her voice dropped in pitch.

'It will not be any more terrifying than what you endured last night,' he replied.

'How can you be so sure?' she countered. 'I have heard nothing of the place. Have you? How do we know what we are getting into?' Her voice was closer now, and soon she was walking alongside him, as the path widened out as they descended the valley and headed towards the river.

Would telling her the truth scare her or help their cause? Rolf wasn't sure. He couldn't get a good read on the woman. She stared up at him with expectation. He decided on sharing *some* truth, since he was already telling her so many lies.

'While I've heard stories and gossip about the place, I've never been there.' Catriona's sister-in-law, Brenna MacLean, and her husband, Laird Garrick MacLean, had once stumbled upon it along their journeys years before, and had found the people kind, but Rolf couldn't risk telling Miss Hay such details. Then he would have even more lies to keep up with, for she would ask how he knew the MacLeans, and he was having difficulty keeping up with the lies he had already told her.

'What kinds of stories?'

'That the village is comprised of a collection of men and women who have lost their own clans to war and starvation. That they escaped and banded together to build their own new community, one where multiple clans can thrive and live peacefully with one another.'

'Hmm. It sounds like a fairy tale,' she murmured.

He scoffed. 'We shall see if it is as idyllic as it sounds. I cannot imagine they do not have struggles with maintaining order and peace, with so many different people and clans in one place, especially if they have all suffered great losses.'

'Perhaps we will be surprised in the best way possible.' She paused. 'Although, I am dreading seeing my mother,' she added.

Her words took on a solemn tone, and Rolf couldn't help but cast a sympathetic glance her way. 'Perhaps she will surprise you in the best way possible too,' he offered.

She bit her lip and crossed her arms against her chest. 'I cannot fathom her abandoning us by choice and my father allowing me to believe her dead all this time. For over a decade, I have grieved and believed the worst of her. Now, I am just angry and confused at them both. I do not understand any of it.'

'Maybe she will give you the answers you seek,' he said.

'I am not sure I want them,' she replied.

He chuckled. 'I understand that too.'

'Do you?' she asked. She could not hide the surprise in her voice and stopped walking. 'How?'

Fool.

He fought the urge to smack himself on the side of the head. *Curses.* Why had he said that? Now he would have to explain how he understood her agony, which was the last thing he wanted to do. She stared up at him with her beautiful, wide, expectant eyes. There was no going back now.

'My parents kept many secrets from me and my siblings, most of which we didn't find out about until they had died. Truthfully, I am still trying to uncover some of them and I…' He paused. 'And I fear I may not like what I find.' A rush of relief pumped through his blood, such as when he ran headlong across an open field, or rode full out on his favourite stallion. Sharing his need to find answers and his fear over what he might discover with someone else besides his siblings made him feel weightless. For just a moment, the shame lifted and he felt…alive.

A twig snapped nearby; he stretched out his right arm to halt her advance and then froze. He listened, surveying the area around them. He breathed in, hoping to smell whatever it was that was close. Was it an animal? A man? Both, perhaps? He'd thought they were alone when they had set out, as he had not seen anything along their horizon, but it was dawn now. They had veered from the open expanse of the valley and were approaching the woods again. The trickle of the half-frozen river was just below. Someone else must have awoken as they had and set out along their own journey, which was about to intersect with theirs.

Another branch snapped and Rolf turned to his left. Whoever it was, they were far closer than he would have liked and might well have spotted them before he heard their approach. He cursed himself. The danger was close—too close. He had allowed himself to be distracted by his conversation with Miss Hay and put them at risk. Another branch snapped. The strangers had made no attempt to disguise their approach, which didn't bode well. Gooseflesh rose along his skin.

'Someone comes. Bind up your hair—now,' Rolf commanded in low tones, heeding his own internal warnings. He scanned the woods, his hand resting upon the dagger on his waist-belt.

Kenna paled, but hastily followed his orders without complaint, tucking her hair beneath her woollen hat and pulling the collar of her jacket high along her neck.

Soon, two men came out of the woods that bordered the path they were following. They appeared to be soldiers from the night before. There was no mistaking it in their stance, posture and soot-smeared cheeks. Blood stained the tartan of the larger of the two men, and the clothes on the other man hung loosely, too loosely, as if they were not his own…much like Miss Hay's.

Deuces.

For all he knew, they could be British soldiers pretending to be fellow Jacobite sympathisers. He'd seen it more than once when he had fought in battle.

'Morn,' one of them said in a strong Scottish burr, with a nod. 'Glad to see others escaped.' The largest of the two strangers studied them in silence, his eyes lingering longer than necessary on Miss Hay's face before drifting along her full form.

Rolf pulled back his shoulders and his jaw tightened. Her ruse was of no use with these men. They knew she was a woman, and they would use it against him. But there was no need to let them know he was aware of their intentions yet. He still hadn't decided if they were friend or foe, and he would know his enemy before he felled them.

'How many others escaped?' Rolf asked, holding the smaller man's gaze, for a man's eyes revealed everything.

The man dropped his gaze and then flicked it back up to Rolf with a sneer. 'Far more than I would have liked,' he growled, his Scottish burr replaced with the sharp, flat tones of a British native. He pulled his blade quickly.

'Run!' Rolf shouted to Miss Hay. The best option the woman had to survive was to run. She was fast and smart, and the smaller of the two men would be encumbered by his oversized clothes... just as she would be.

Curses. He needed to fell the larger man quickly before he could assist her. While he loathed killing, he found he was quite skilled at it once he set his mind to it. And keeping Miss Hay safe was all he wanted to do now. He drew his own blade and lowered his stance, moving in a rhythm that mirrored the other man's own. Impatient, the other man lunged, which was exactly what Rolf had hoped for. He blocked the man's blade and sunk his own deep into the man's gut before twisting it and pulling it out with force. The man's eyes widened in shock as he dropped his blade and fell to his knees.

This was the part Rolf did not like. He would leave the man to die alone and live with the burden of knowing he had taken a life. But what choice had he had? Rolf turned and examined the area behind him, straining for any sign of which direction Miss Hay and the other soldier had gone. The grass left no clues for him. He decided to retrace their journey. Miss Hay might have run in that direction on instinct, since it was the only way she knew. He started to jog in that direction and prayed he was right.

The echo of Miss Hay's scream through the woods and the eerie silence that followed sent a chill through his veins. He'd been wrong. He skidded to a stop and doubled back, running at a full sprint in the direction of her scream, his boots skimming off the harsh ground and over fallen trees and boulders. Finally, he saw the horrid man looming over her still form. Blood ran from the side of her head. The man had ripped off her jacket and tartan and straddled her tiny form. His intent was obvious and the mere thought of him interfering with the lass made Rolf's blood rage. He ploughed into the man, tackling him to the ground at full speed.

The stranger was small, but thick and brutal, his fists connecting with Rolf's torso. Rolf yelled in fury, consumed by the image of Miss Hay on the ground and his failure to protect her. He pinned the attacker to the ground and landed punch after punch to his face.

'Yield!' he yelled to the man, trying to prevent yet another death, but the man smiled at him and reached for his blade.

Rolf cursed and crushed the man's wrist before slamming the back of his head on the frozen ground. Finally, the man stilled: he was dead. Rolf sat back on his haunches, panting for breath, his hands and torso shaking as fury and mania coursed through his body. He closed his eyes and took deep breaths, attempting to regain his control.

His brother, Royce, had taught Rolf many skills, and the others he had learned during his brief stint with the Jacobite army before he'd realised he didn't have the stomach for such a cause.

You may not have the heart of a warrior, brother, but you have the skill of an assassin. Royce's words echoed in Rolf's mind and brought him back to the present. He'd had no choice. It had been either Miss Hay or these men, and her life outweighed both of theirs.

Miss Hay let out a small gasp behind him, and

Rolf turned to see her sitting up. Her hand covered her mouth and her eyes were wide with terror. Rolf shifted to the side to try to shield her view of the dead soldier behind him, but he had little luck. Her hand fell away from her mouth, and she stared past him.

'Is he dead?' she asked as a tear fell down her cheek.

'Aye,' he said, feeling a mixture of shame and relief over what he had done to protect her. He stood and walked over to her. He offered her his hand to help her up.

After a moment, she finally looked away from the dead man and her shaking hand clutched Rolf's. The strength of her cool, fluttering grip surprised him, and he wrapped his hand tightly around it. When he pulled her up to stand, she threw her body against him, holding him with a desperate urgency that frightened him. He stiffened. At first, he didn't put his hands around her. He wasn't sure what he should do. But, as she clung to him with her slight but strong form shivering against his own, he did the only thing he knew was right: he eased his arms around her, held her just as tightly and murmured in her ear, 'It will be all right, love. I promise.'

It didn't matter if he might be outright lying to

her. They might not survive their journey or reach the Lost Village unscathed, but in this moment he needed to console her as he needed to console himself. The imminent danger of minutes ago had passed. She was safe.

For long minutes, they held each other and a part of Rolf, long hidden and long frozen, began to thaw. The feel of a woman against him needing him in such a way made him feel alive, more alive than he'd felt in such a long time. To be wanted, to be needed and to be held as if he mattered made him falter. He swallowed hard.

'Thank you,' she murmured against his throat, followed by a small hiccup. She eased back to see his face. Her sea-green gaze pulled him in like the hypnotic rhythm of waves crashing against the shore, and he found himself unable to look away.

He brushed the rogue strands that had fallen from her braid back behind her ear, the top of which was so soft and tender…just like her. She trembled against his touch and then she leaned in and kissed him. The first delicate caress of her lips fell upon his cheek and then his mouth, tentatively at first, and then with a certainty that shocked him. He responded to her in kind, kissing her thoroughly and with all the emotion and relief he felt in her being alive and mostly unharmed…and in being needed. Needed by someone who wasn't family and by someone who didn't even know he was a Cameron.

Then he realised what he was doing and pulled back. 'Apologies,' he muttered, trying to distance himself a bit, but reluctant to pull away entirely.

Saints be. What was he doing? He needed to protect her, not bed her. He felt as small as a flea on a cow.

Her cheeks pinked. 'Nay. It was me, I...' She looked away, pressed her lips together and then stepped back out of their embrace. She touched her head and looked at the blood on her fingers.

'Is this mine?' she asked, the colour draining from her face.

'Aye,' he answered. 'Let me.' He tore a swatch from his plaid and dabbed her temple. She winced but didn't resist. 'Are you dizzy? Confused? Does your head hurt?' he asked.

'Aye,' she replied. 'But only from all of your questions,' she added with a smirk. 'I am a bit dizzy, but mostly stunned. You saved my life. Thank you.'

He stilled, reluctant to accept her appreciation. He squared his shoulders.

'Nay. I don't deserve it. My recklessness almost got you killed. If I'd been paying better attention, they wouldn't have taken us by surprise.' He stared down at her lips, remembering the kiss they'd shared and the fire it had kindled within him, and tried to smother it out. 'It won't happen again.' He grabbed her coat from the ground and handed it to her.

She accepted it, but confusion registered in her features.

'We must go,' he added hastily, his gaze searching their surroundings. 'There may be more of them.'

Chapter Five

Fool.

Kenna should have put her coat back on, but she clutched it close to her chest instead as they began to head back to the trail they had followed before they'd been attacked by the British soldiers.

She fell in step behind Mr Dunbar. What had she been thinking? Her cheeks heated and she pressed her lips together. This man was here to protect her, and she had no right to kiss him and complicate matters. He could be married. Her stomach lurched. He might even have children. Why had she never asked? Why had she assumed that he was alone and unattached, like her? Probably because he acted like an unattached man: a wolf; a loner; a man unused to complications and entanglements. In some ways, his loneliness reminded her of herself.

She frowned and watched him climb. And yet, his steps and every movement about him were so... certain, so assured and so unapologetic. Unlike her; her life had been one uncertain step after another after her mother had left when she'd been a child. She'd done her best to hide from everyone, hadn't she? It was safer to be alone and not risk further rejection or loss. If her mother couldn't love her, who could? Kenna felt that even more keenly now, knowing, after having believed her dead for so long, her mother had not only abandoned her but was still alive. And the idea of having to explain her gift of the runes to a stranger made Kenna's stomach churn. She would not allow herself to be ridiculed about something that was such a precious and essential part of who she was.

Nay, it was best to be alone and keep herself hidden.

Her gaze fell upon Mr Dunbar once more.

But this man was bold, skilled, and oozed confidence, which she envied. He was also ridiculously handsome. She had tried to pretend that she didn't notice the sheer power and ferocity of his form every time he moved, but it was impossible not to. He was tall, muscular, and had brutal strength, based on what had remained of the two men who had attacked them. She shivered at the memory of their still forms, despite the heat and energy still buzzing through her body from when she and Mr Dunbar had kissed.

Yet when she'd seen him looking over at the dead man, when he'd thought her to be unconscious, he had seemed haunted and uncertain, just as he had the moment before he responded to her kiss. None of it made sense to her. Neither did he. But, in truth, she hadn't known many men her own age. Most men who frequented her father's antique shop were older and friends of her father. Maybe all men acted this way. How was she to know? She shrugged on her coat and flushed. She pressed her fingertips to her lips. Although *she* had enjoyed their kiss, perhaps it had been lacking. She had all but thrown herself at him after the attack, and she had only ever kissed one boy before. And that had been, well, rather forgettable.

But Mr Dunbar *had* kissed her back. She had felt the pressure and intensity of his lips on hers down to the tips of her chilled toes. His touch had elicited a slow thaw in her body. She twisted her lips and frowned. Now she was even more confused.

'Keep up,' he called back. She picked up her

pace and studied his back. Had he kissed her back out of kindness, or some sense of duty or obligation, since he was bound to protect her and had been compensated by her father to do so? Shame lanced through her, and she thought she might burst into flame. Surely not? She couldn't have mistaken his response that much. He'd seemed to enjoy it, had he not?

She shook her head. *Blast.* She was turning into one of those daft lasses she overheard at the market square who prattled on and on about this boy or that boy. But Mr Dunbar was no boy, was he? He was a man, a soldier, a killer. He was also her protector.

Her heart fluttered in her chest. And he had saved her life. Perhaps the rogue kiss didn't matter after all. She'd been emotional and reacting to almost having died. Surely that counted for something? Most likely the kiss would be easily forgotten by Mr Dunbar, so she might as well treat it the same. They would be parting company once they reached Loch's End. He would have fulfilled his contract with her father, and she would have kept her promise to him as well. In a fortnight or less, they would be out of each other's lives for good. They would be mere memories to each other, would they not?

She clutched the satchel of runes along her waist. They would know. The runes always knew. Her fingers itched with uncertainty as she turned the stones over and over within the cloth bag, the rhythmic movements calming her as they climbed the valley and spied the snow-covered mountains ahead. The sun began its rugged climb higher in the sky. The thick clouds from before were clearing to reveal a hypnotic bird's-egg-blue horizon. Her head throbbed in time with her steps, and she squinted, pressing her fingers to her temple. At least the bleeding had lessened, even if it hadn't stopped entirely, despite the bandages Mr Dunbar had wrapped around her head.

She skidded on a small patch of ice but regained her footing. He paused and turned to her. He studied her with concern and waited for her to reach his side, where she stopped next to him.

'Your head?' he asked, his gaze drifting to the plaid wrap briefly before meeting her eyes.

'Aching,' she replied, 'but I can continue.' She couldn't quite muster a smile. She was weary and it was still early. The day would be long.

'Once we make the ridge, you can rest. Some sleep may help ease the ache.' He turned off the worn trail and continued walking. She fell in step behind him, climbing over brush and a few fallen branches.

His pace picked up as they entered a section of woodlands lightly dusted with new snow, and his hand never left the hilt of the blade tucked into his waist-belt. He was worried about something. Her, perhaps, or other soldiers following them? She scanned the remote terrain. While it looked undisturbed, it was hard to know for sure. It was a mixture of lush evergreens and naked hardwoods whose limbs reached into the sky, longing for their own glimpse of the warm sun.

She smiled when she recognised the familiar tracks of a hare and the odd imprint of the fox that would have followed it in pursuit of its first meal of the day. Her mother had taught her how to identify them in a patch of woods like this long ago when she'd been a wee girl with lopsided braids. While her father had been in his shop or tinkering with the repairs of an old antique he hoped to salvage, Kenna and her mother had had adventures in the woods or explored the secrets of the runes. Kenna had cherished those adventures with her mother until thcy had abruptly stopped without any explanation or warning. One morn, her mother had simply gone.

'And what adventure are ye on this morn, wee

girl?' Bridget had asked her, plopping a spoonful of cooked oats in her bowl, followed by a chunk of bread with butter.

'We are off to the caves,' Kenna had answered, her legs swinging back and forth under the table. She'd taken a huge bite of bread, smearing the butter on her cheek. She'd laughed as she tried to lick it off.

'Lass, what shall I do with ye?' Bridget had chided with a smile before wiping Kenna's cheek with the edge of her apron.

Kenna had chuckled and had a spoonful of oats, the warmth coating her belly, and the touch of jam dabbed on it tasting sweet in her mouth. She'd savoured it before swallowing it down.

'What do you think we shall find in the caves?' Kenna had asked.

'Bats, most likely,' Bridget had teased.

'Ew! Not bats. Mother would not take me to such a place.'

Her father had entered the room, holding his hat in his hand.

'You won't be going anywhere this morn, my girl.' His words had sounded flat and heavy.

They'd both turned to him.

'Why?' Kenna had asked. 'Is Mother ill?'

'Nay,' he'd answered simply. 'She is gone.'

Even now warm, cooked oats curdled her stomach. The smell, taste and mere thought of them set her gut upside down.

Gone.

The way her father had said the word had sounded like a hammer hitting an anvil: certain; permanent; for ever.

So for Kenna to know she was heading to see the woman who had abandoned her so long ago seemed surreal and like a dream she could not wake from but wished to. Kenna half-expected to arrive at the Lost Village and see her mother and father both there, standing side by side holding hands, as they had when she'd been a child. But she knew that was not real. Her father was dead. Her mother was a liar.

She was alone, except for Mr Dunbar.

And Bridget. The poor woman was no doubt fraught with worry, with Kenna gone, but she'd had no choice. Fulfilling Father's wish was paramount. Once she did so, Kenna could return home, and she and Bridget could work out what was next for them both. Life stopped for no one, not even for the grieving.

She smiled down at her father's clothes. They hung off her body, as if she were playing pretend, which she was, but they comforted her. The jacket still smelled of him. She brought the sleeve up to her nose and inhaled the familiar mint and tallow. Her eyes watered. She still didn't understand why he'd been killed. Such a waste of a life to protect the secrets of a family he did not know.

The Camerons. She despised them already and she would tell them so once she reached them. She wrapped her hand around one small sapling and then another to steady herself as she climbed. It was steeper now, and she had to concentrate to keep her footing.

Mr Dunbar had not spoken for an age, but Kenna didn't mind. The quiet between them suited her even if it thrust her mind into incessant thought. They continued until the sun was right overhead, a reminder that it was midday. Her stomach rumbled.

Mr Dunbar cast a glance back at her and then branched out of the woods towards a small cave.

'We will stop here, rest and eat. Then we will continue to the ridge.' He pointed off to the west. 'According to the maps, there is an abandoned church there. We can stay there for the night. We should then reach the village.' He studied her and waited.

'Aye,' she replied in a rush. She didn't realise he had been awaiting a response.

'You are pale.'

She shrugged. 'Cold. Tired. Hungry.' That was the best she could do. She swayed and he clutched her arm and led her to the mouth of the cave.

'Wait here,' he said, before letting go of her arm and disappearing into the darkness. Shortly after, he returned. He guided her to a boulder that was slightly elevated from the ground. 'Rest here.'

The moment she sat upon it, she sighed and closed her eyes. Fatigue was closing in like a warm blanket. He guided her upper torso back to lie down, and she let him, all efforts to resist sleep abandoned. Despite how hard the boulder was, at least she was no longer moving. The stillness soothed her, and the ache at her temple lessened. He tucked something soft under her head and she sighed. 'Thank you,' she murmured, before curling up and falling into a deep slumber.

Rolf scrubbed a hand through his hair as he stood at the mouth of the cave watching Miss Hay sleep. *Saints be.* He didn't know what to make of her. His charge was supposed to be just that; a task. He was meant to bring her to the Lost Village, meet with the lass's mother, get the information he sought, convince her to stay with her mother and then travel on to Loch's End alone. But here he was. The woman was injured, they were most likely being pursued by British soldiers and he had little idea if the Lost Village was really where Hay had denoted it on the map.

Nothing had gone to plan, which angered him to his core. Why could nothing in his life be simple or true? Why did everything come with so many complications?

He stared upon Miss Hay's fragile form, her delicate face and soft, parted lips. The one thing that hadn't felt complicated was their kiss. It had been simple and true, and had come from a rush of feeling and relief from being alive, from having survived a moment that could have ended them both.

But, after that moment had passed between them, he'd felt like a rake. She was vulnerable, and he knew that. He shouldn't have returned her attentions with such…vigour. But she was so lovely… and the way she had looked upon him had made him feel like a greater man than he was, like the very man he wished to be. And he didn't regret kissing her, not really. Deep down, he knew he *should* have regrets, but he didn't, and if given the chance again he would do the same. So, he would accept he was a rake and move on. Too much was at stake now.

Even in sleep, her hand held the small satchel along her waist. He wondered what exactly she was so protective of. He'd seen her turn the contents within it and it seemed to soothe her. He walked over and studied her. What other secrets did she hide? He scanned her form and noted the large sewn inner pocket of her jacket that was slightly exposed to him. Something was still in that pocket other than the letters she had shown him. It had the outline of a book.

He frowned and bent closer. She'd not told him of any book. He eased his hand over her slowly, skimming her hip, and she shifted towards him. He stilled and let her settle back to sleep. His hand rested on her hip. A flash of the want he'd felt for her earlier ignited again and his pulse increased.

Steady.

After another minute, he dared to reach into the pocket once more. He held his breath, pressing his lips together, and allowed his hand to glide over her lower back to the pocket. He wriggled as many fingers as he could in the space until he felt a smooth, cool leather cover. He clamped his fingers around it and tugged it free as gently as he could. The bound book slid out of the pocket, and he let it glide along her back and hip slowly. He prayed she wouldn't wake, and his prayers were answered. Once he backed away from her, and stepped out of the mouth of the cave to the full light of the sun, he examined it.

The bound book was old, very old. The edges of the leather were worn smooth by years or perhaps decades of use and the pages were sewn together by thick lacing along the binding. The cover had intricate relief designs. The designs looked Scottish at first glance, but when he studied it closer it looked far more Gaelic, perhaps even Nordic. And the symbols... He almost dropped the book to the ground as a flash of a childhood memory overtook him. A memory that had woken him multiple times in his sleep as a vivid dream since the first of Bartholomew Hay's letters had arrived.

The doors to the library had been closed with haste. 'What are you doing here?' his mother had snapped at a man Rolf had not known. 'How did you even get in? You will be killed if you are discovered.'

''Tis worth the risk, and I have my ways. With you, I am inspired to be creative,' the man had answered, his Scottish burr rolling deeply. Rolf had not recognised the voice.

'Stop,' his mother had begged. 'What happened years ago was a mistake. It shall not happen again.'

'Nay. It was no mistake,' the man had said. 'And my wife is dead. Leave him. Be with me.'

'I cannot. I will not,' she'd replied.

'Then I shall tell him of your betrayal.'

'You will do no such thing. I will claim you forced yourself on me, and he will believe me.'

Her words had been harsh, and their brutality had shocked him. The carved wooden wolf figurine Rolf had been holding had clattered to the floor.

'Someone is here,' she'd whispered. 'I must go. So must you.'

'You cannot leave me,' the man had commanded. 'Not yet. Not now.'

'I must,' his mother had said. 'This must cease…'

'Nay. He does not know. He is a fool. And you…' His voice had dropped. 'I know you love me more.'

His mother had whimpered. 'Stop. You're hurting me.'

'Mother!' Rolf had called, rushing from behind the row of books where he had been hiding.

As he'd reached the edge, Rolf had seen a glimpse of his mother's face. A hand had slapped the side of his head hard, and he'd crumpled to the floor as the spinning world had come to a dark and silent stop.

Rolf jolted and sucked in a breath. That was as

much as he could ever remember. Each time the memory was as sharp and clear as if it had just happened and his heart clunked irregularly in his chest. The terrified boy in him remembered that interaction with a stranger from decades ago, but the man he was now couldn't make sense of it all.

Had the man from his memories been Audric MacDonald? They now knew he was Catriona's real father. His sister's conception and lineage had been something his parents had been desperate to hide. So desperate that they had left his sister alone on Lismore to grow up an orphan and pretended to everyone that she had been lost to the sea.

Rolf's body tightened. The rage over what had befallen his half-sister since his parents' decision came roaring back, not to mention the anger at being denied so many years with her.

But could the man from his memories have been someone else? Surely no other man had been involved with his mother? His stomach knotted.

Deuces.

How would he ever know, and did he truly want to? His memory always faded on the precipice of seeing the man's face. He closed his eyes and tried to focus on the last moments before his memory was lost. He thought back to the images… Just before the darkness, he'd felt the hit and had seen a man's hand and the edge of his wrist.

Rolf stilled and opened his eyes.

The hand... The wrist... The man had had symbols like the ones on the cover of this book inked along his wrist. He was sure of it now. But it had been a series of them, and only a few of them had been visible, and even the ones he could remember were a bit fuzzy and incomplete. But they'd looked like some of the ones carved into the cover of this book, though none of them looked identical.

He flipped open the book. It was page after page of intricate drawings, detailed maps and dates with symbols. It appeared to be more like a diary than a book. Some pages had line after line of symbols he could not decipher. Some of them looked like the ones he had seen on the man's wrist, but he didn't even know what language it was. He'd never seen it before.

Scraps of parchment with notes on them had been placed throughout the book that he could read. Perhaps someone was deciphering them. Were they codes? His palm rested on a page with three symbols: a slanted H, a capital Y with an added branch in the middle at the top, and what looked like butterfly wings. There were words written beneath each one: *Disruption. Protection. Hope.*

Rolf mumbled the words aloud to himself over and over like a chant. There was something about the order of those words that felt soothing, and he found himself somewhat entranced by them.

His gaze rested on the woman sleeping before him. Had Miss Hay taken these notes and added them in? Or had it been the work of her father? He studied the handwriting again. Nay. The writing was far more distinctive than Bartholomew Hay's and had the added flourishes of a woman's touch. But why had she not told him about this diary? Why keep this hidden when she'd openly shared the maps and letters with him? Why not share this? The notes made as little sense to him as the carvings, so he supposed it didn't entirely matter, although he did need to know why she was withholding information from him. What she knew might be endangering them or keeping them safe. It was hard to tell.

The more he discovered about Miss Kenna Hay, the more he wanted to know. For all her delicate beauty, she was fierce. She'd disguised herself as a man and alone joined a band of Jacobite soldiers to keep a promise to her father.

She stirred and he rushed over to her. He had to return the diary before she knew what he'd done. He leaned over her and started to slip the book back into her coat pocket. Her eyes flashed open and she grabbed his wrist. 'What are you doing?' she demanded.

He turned the tables. 'Reading the diary you have hidden from me, Miss Hay…despite being your protector.' He held her gaze and matched her ire with his own.

She let go of his wrist as if it were fire and sat up quickly, scooting away from him. The fear he saw in her gaze made him regret his accusation and tone. The last thing he wished was for her to be frightened of him.

Her breath was jagged and her chest rose and fell as she watched him as if she expected the worst, like a startled doe waiting for his next move. He sat down on the boulder near her feet and let the book rest on his thigh. 'We will eat, we will continue and, this eve when we are settled, you will tell me what this is and how it relates to our journey. I assume it has great importance, for you to keep it from me.' He extended his hand and nudged the book towards her. 'Take it. It is yours.'

Her uncertainty and silence tugged at him. She

nodded, tentatively reached forward to take it from him and then tucked it back in her coat pocket. He pulled a small pouch from his waist-belt and removed two strips of dried beef for them to eat. 'I know it isn't much, but we cannot risk a fire, and cannot stay long enough to hunt here.' He offered her a piece and she took it. She bit into it and made a face as she chewed, but eventually swallowed it.

He smiled. 'It takes some getting used to.'

She shrugged. 'It is better than cooked oats.'

He was surprised. 'Oh?'

'Aye. I despise them.'

He finished up his piece, dusted off his trews and rose. 'I'll remember that.'

She ate in silence and he kept an eye outside the cave. Everything seemed quiet, and he wasn't sure if he preferred it that way or not. Either way, they needed to move on. 'Feeling better?' he asked.

Miss Hay finished eating, stood up and stretched, letting out a loud yawn. 'Aye. Much. Thank you.'

His gaze flitted down to the pouch tied around her waist. When she noted the direction of his stare, she pulled her coat around her tightly. Whatever she hid from him, it related to that pouch as well, the one she was so protective of. 'Let us go,' he said and headed off with Miss Hay a step behind.

While the lady had her secrets, Rolf knew well that he also had his own.

Chapter Six

Curses.

Kenna followed a stride behind Mr Dunbar, her boots sinking into the snow that had deepened as they'd continued their advance up the side of the mountain. How had the man found the book and how on earth had she not awoken to him removing it from her person?

She hugged the coat tighter around her body, as if it could provide her with the protection she sought. She knew well it couldn't. She wanted a measure of security a mere wool coat could not provide. Mr Dunbar was getting too close to what she was trying so hard to hide from him. She needed to get rid of the man once they reached the Lost Village. He would only complicate matters once he learned of her skills with the runes, and the book with its many maps and runic messages. She had only just begun to analyse it. To have it taken from her now would end her journey to the truth before it had begun. And her father deserved better. His death would not be in vain—not if she had any say in the matter.

But Mr Dunbar had been a man of his word. He had not spoken a syllable about the book or her deception since they'd left the cave. Hours had passed since they'd set out north and west, or at least it felt that way. She was not a good judge of time and distance on the best of days, let alone now, after a mild head injury. It seemed an eternity had passed between this morn and now, much of which she would have liked to forget.

Except for their kiss, maybe. She had no desire to forget that part.

Off in the distance, she spied movement dotting the hillsides in the shadows of the afternoon sun. Dusk would be upon them soon. She squinted and her shoulders relaxed. It was merely a smattering of Highland cows roaming and having their fill. The creatures were adept at finding food and vegetation beneath the snow. Kenna's stomach grumbled. She was jealous of their success. The piece of dried beef was the only food she had consumed since she'd met Mr Dunbar and her body's dull ache was a testimony to the strains of the day and the nourishment she lacked.

'The abandoned church on the map should be on the other side of that hill,' he stated.

She said nothing in reply but continued, taking one plodding step after another, following in the divots his steps had made to prevent more of the snow from seeping into her boots. She turned the runes in her pouch for comfort. The weight of the word 'should' was not as encouraging as she would have liked, but she couldn't begrudge him. They were following a hastily drawn old map, from what he'd said. Its markers could have changed, and she could not hold the man responsible for that even if she would like to. It was far easier to be cross with him; that way, he wasn't so attractive.

The sharp, high-pitched bellow of one of the Highland cows seized Kenna's attention. Mr Dunbar slowed and held out his arm to guard her. He scanned the hillside and the same cow let out the same plaintive moo, and then another cow echoed it.

'Come with me,' he ordered and clutched her hand in his own, half-dragging her into the edge of the brush and evergreens that lined the hillside. 'Something is amiss. Even the cows know it.'

'Are you saying those cows just warned us?' Kenna whispered as she rushed alongside him, kicking up snow in their wake as they half-slid down a patch of the slope.

'Aye.'

She chuckled. 'You speak cow?'

'Aye. I spent many a day in the fields when I was young, after my mother died.' He turned back and briefly scanned the woods for danger before they continued.

She blinked at him. The man was serious. He'd also just revealed something personal. She didn't know which she was more surprised by.

'That is a warning from a distressed cow—something is close by. Could be a predator or a person unknown to them. Either way, I have no wish to find out. We will go around.'

'A warning?' she murmured. She settled into silence and kept pace with him as they crossed the last patch of forest and ended up close to the edge of the trail again. Before they reached it, they heard voices. He clutched her arm and they halted, rooted to their spots, listening.

'The ol' girl is never wrong,' a woman said, her voice raspy with age. 'Someone was 'ere.'

'I see no one, Flora. I've combed through the fold. If there was someone or something there, they've gone,' a younger man answered, unable to hide his annoyance.

'Pfft,' she replied. 'Ye will see. Never wrong, I tell ye, never.'

'I'm heading back to the village. Doran needs me for some real work.'

'Real work,' the older woman mimicked.

Kenna covered her mouth to smother a smile. She admired the older woman's pluck.

Once the pair had moved on and disappeared up and over the bend, Mr Dunbar retrieved his map and studied it. His brow was furrowed as he smoothed out the worn parchment against his thigh and tried to gather the lingering light of dusk to examine it. 'According to this, we shouldn't be at the Lost Village yet, but…'

'I noted the different plaids as well,' Kenna offered. 'They were not from the same clans, yet they travelled back together to what appeared to be *their* village. And they playfully disagreed, as if they knew each other well.'

He sighed and his shoulders dropped. 'I agree.

My gut says it's the place, even if the map doesn't suggest it. You?'

His gaze searched hers. The shock of him asking her advice stunned her and she didn't answer immediately. Did he value her opinion? Did he value her? The idea that he did made her stomach flutter just as when they'd kissed. She bit her lip and studied the area around them. 'May I see?' she asked, gesturing to the map.

He handed it to her. 'According to this, we shouldn't be so close,' he explained, pointing to the map. 'We should have a day more before the village comes in sight. We should be coming upon this abandoned church here.'

Kenna turned the map and shifted it. 'How can you be so sure of the orientation?'

He paused and studied it. 'I assumed it by where the compass is drawn upon it, as with most maps.' He pointed to the small directional guide on the bottom right.

She smiled, studying the map more closely. 'Father,' she murmured, running her hand over it before turning it. 'Well, Mr Dunbar, this map was drawn by my father, who preferred his compass to be on the upper left.'

'What?' He stared at it again. 'How is that possible? How can you tell what is land or sea?'

'He used these small wave-like arrows even though he used no other signifier. I can see how you believed it flipped. I have spent many years looking at his maps. They often only made sense to him.' She chuckled and a small pull of memory tugged at her.

'Why did you not tell me I had the map upside down?' He huffed, unable to disguise his frustration.

She balked and met his ire. 'You did not ask, and I did not think to question your map-reading skills. You are my protector, are you not?' she answered, challenging him.

His face fell into a scowl. 'Let us go, then. The village and some much-needed rest await.'

She rolled her eyes and fell into step behind him, following the moulds of his tracks in the snow as before. Suddenly, her nerves kicked in and she was unsteady on her feet. While she was ready to *see* the village, and accept the comforts of a warm blanket and a hot meal, she wasn't ready to see her mother. While Kenna had ignored the idea of their possible reunion for most of the journey, she had no more time to postpone the thought of it. The time had come, and she didn't feel the least bit prepared. She didn't know if she could expect a warm reception from her. She might be dead; it had been over a decade. Father could have been wrong.

Or she could reject her all over again. Kenna's stomach soured; the previous hunger turned to nausea, and she tripped over a rock. Mr Dunbar caught her by the forearm and steadied her. He held her arm as they continued the sharp ascent.

'No matter what you feel when you see her,' he offered in soft tones, 'she is your mother—your *only* mother. Offer what kindness you can, even if you feel she doesn't deserve it.'

She met his gaze, full of softness now rather than ire, and her eyes burned hot with sudden tears. Glancing away, she blinked them back. How had he known what she was thinking? It was un-nerving.

'I will speak first,' he said as they neared a wider and much more worn path, wide enough for carriages and horses to pass. 'If they become hostile, just run. I will give you time to escape.'

'And then what?' she asked, startled by the sudden shift in topic and the new fear of being attacked scrambling her reason.

He shrugged. 'Most likely I will be dead, but you are smart. You will continue without me.'

'Very encouraging,' she muttered as they approached the outskirts of a small village. Well-kept cottages and tidy pens with animals were nestled snugly side by side and a few men and women stared at them as they approached the edge of the first cottage.

The men standing guard enclosed them quickly, and soon all Kenna could hear was the voice in her head commanding her to run. Mr Dunbar edged closer to her, his shoulder touching her own and the back of his hand skimming hers. In his own way, he was trying to comfort her. Unfortunately, it didn't work. Her heart hammered in her chest and her throat dried.

'Who are you?' the older of the guards asked, studying them closely, although most of his attention was on Mr Dunbar, as he no doubt posed the greater threat.

'We will speak to the person in charge,' Mr Dunbar demanded. His gaze was unflinching, his body tense. Kenna held her breath.

'You will speak with me,' the guard countered.

'Nay. We will wait. Let him know we are here.' That brutality from before returned, and Mr Dunbar became someone else, someone cold, detached and ready to kill to protect her. She commanded herself not to flinch, but to be as still and as certain as him. She let out a shaky breath but held the other guard's gaze. She would handle herself if she had to, and by 'handle herself' she meant run—run for her life.

'Tell Doran of our...*guests*,' the older guard ordered, relenting to Mr Dunbar's demands. The other man jogged off to the village and Kenna's gaze followed his direction, taking the opportunity to take in their surroundings. Even though nightfall was pressing tightly around them, the village appeared to be thriving. The animals and people were well cared for, from what she could see, and cottages sprawled through the sprinkling of trees and woods for as far as the trees would allow. This Lost Village appeared anything but lost. They seemed to have found a footing and a life outside the traditional clan system.

Kenna was absolutely intrigued by it. So far, she had counted five different plaids, and she'd only begun her inspection. How did they manage it?

Within a few minutes, a man approached them, flanked by additional guards. He had to be the leader of the village; he had an imposing way about him the others responded to. He was tall with a medium build and thick brown hair that shielded most of his eyes. Scars slashed his left cheek, marring an otherwise perfect face. Despite it, the man was attractive, and the scars made him even more formidable. He studied Mr Dunbar as he walked, no doubt assessing who they might be and why they might be here.

The man stopped at arm's length, his guards a step closer, and just as he began to speak his eyes flicked over to Kenna. He stilled, arrested by the sight of her, and his mouth closed. A blush heated her cheeks. His intense assessment of her was unnerving. She shifted on her feet but held his gaze, unwilling to lose whatever challenge this was.

'My apologies,' he muttered as he recovered himself. A wistful smile softened his features and he looked boyish for a moment. 'You look so much like someone I used to know.' He cleared his throat and refocused his energy on Mr Dunbar.

She said nothing. What did one say to such a thing? How could they possibly have known one another?

'Kenna?'

Mother. She would have known her voice anywhere.

The knot of unease in Kenna's gut fell away and she turned her head, searching for her mother amongst the growing sea of villagers that had emerged to see who dared arrive in the manner they had, unannounced and with the demands to see their leader without explaining who they were.

At first, Kenna didn't recognise her mother. She

was thinner than before, and her hair was a grey knot at the base of her neck. 'Mother!' Kenna cried and rushed to her, despite Mr Dunbar's gentle tug upon her arm to wait. It had been over a decade. She would waste no more time. The anger at being left and being deceived fell away in a way she hadn't expected. All Kenna wanted was to hold her mother and to be held by her once more, just as she wished for her father. But that chance was long gone.

Only her mother remained. They each wove through the onlookers to reach each other and embraced. Gone were her mother's once lush, soft hugs. She was thin, almost too much so, and the feel of her fragile, tiny frame in Kenna's arms surprised her more than all else. But the familiar smell of sage and lavender enveloped her, just like the sweet murmurings of her mother's long-lost affection in her ear. Tears streamed unbidden down their cheeks, and they cried in one another's arms.

This was her *mother*—the one lost to her for so long—found in a place where lost things hid themselves. Kenna's heart was full, full of hope, for the first time since her father's death. She was not alone in the world. She had Bridget, she had

Mr Dunbar and now…now she had her mother back. If only she could say the same for her father.

When Kenna pulled back to take a good look at her mother, she knew with all she was that her thinner frame was not only due to age but sickness. There was no disguising her mother's sunken cheeks or lack of colour in her face. Seeing her daughter should have brought a flush of colour to her face but it hadn't. The joy Kenna had felt moments ago faded.

'Are you ill?' Kenna asked before she could think better of it. She ran a hand down her mother's hair. It was no longer silken and smooth, but brittle and coarse, and her once-plump skin was weathered and dry.

Worry crossed her mother's features and then she sighed. 'Aye. But seeing you once more has brought me peace about it. Knowing you are here now, my beautiful girl, eases all my suffering. You shall guide us all through this. How did you even know to come? Or where I was?' She leaned forward and dropped her voice. 'Was it the runes?'

'Nay,' Kenna answered quietly, noting the crowd of people now shifting towards them. 'Perhaps we could go somewhere and talk properly,' she suggested, hoping to remove themselves from all the prying ears and eyes around them.

'Of course,' she agreed. 'You must be exhausted. Come; you can change, warm yourself and we will put on a pot of stew. Flora will not believe it.'

'Aunt Flora?' Kenna rocked to a halt.

'Aye. She is here too.'

Kenna stood frozen. She had thought her aunt lived far away up north and that was why her father had not visited her recently. It was too much to take in.

'Bring your friend too, if you like. A tall one, that one,' she offered, and winked at Kenna.

Blast. She'd almost forgotten him in all the commotion. She craned her neck and spotted him easily in the crowd as he towered over most of the men there.

'Mr Dunbar!' she called over the people between them. He was deep in discussions with the man who'd believed her to be someone he knew. They both paused and looked up. Mr Dunbar spotted her and she waved him over. He shook the other man's hand and jogged over to her. The other man continued to stare at her, haunted by what he saw, it seemed. Was he another long-lost relative too? He didn't look familiar to her at all.

No matter. She would work it out later. For once, time and luck seemed to be on their side.

'Mother, this is Mr Dunbar. He is my…' Kenna

paused, wondering how to explain it. 'My protector. He is accompanying me at Father's request.'

Her mother studied the man without a word.

'Mr Dunbar, this is Dierdre Hay. My mother.' Saying her mother's first name out loud felt strangled and strange, yet somehow beautiful. She had missed saying it. She had missed so many things about her mother and so much time with her. Kenna pushed down the sadness welling up in her. There would be time to be sad later, but not now.

'Thank you for caring for her, Mr Dunbar,' her mother offered. 'Please, both of you follow me to get a hot meal, change of clothes and to warm by the fire. Our cottage is just here.'

'We would be grateful for such, Mrs Hay. Thank you,' he replied.

''Tis settled, then. Follow me.'

To her surprise, Mr Dunbar shifted his gaze to Kenna as they walked. 'I am pleased to see you reunited and happy, Miss Hay.' He smiled and squeezed her hand briefly before letting go. His kindness and touch made her giddy. He said nothing else as they walked side by side, and she was grateful for it. Her emotions were roiling and confusing as it was, without the complication of his kindness and care to muddle the evening further.

Dierdre Hay's cottage was as pristine within

as it was without, and it made Kenna smile. Everything was in its place, and Kenna breathed in the fragrant, smoky scents of the fire and the bubbling stew of meat and vegetables. Several pots and handmade carvings were tucked in cosy shelves and each nook was filled with an item of beauty as well as use. Her mother had always been precise and exacting in this way, always in stark contrast to the wild and haphazard way her father had gone through life. Her father had been disorganised, often dishevelled, but bubbling over with joy. Her mother had been orderly, structured and purposeful—well, in most ways. With the runes, she was different. With them, she was open to interpretation and embraced the chaos and uncertainty, for the runes spoke differently to everyone, and not always in a place and time that was convenient.

Her mother closed the door behind them and Kenna spied a satchel of runes identical to hers secured to her waist. This was one of the ways they were bonded: by their gifts with the runes. While Kenna was a gifted rune caster, her mother was an incredible one. Finally, Kenna would be able to ask her mother all the questions she had about them and how to use them properly.

'Flora,' her mother called. 'We've company.'

'The stew is almost done. Why did ye not tell me? I didn'a make enough,' the woman complained, her voice matching that of the old woman they'd first overheard on the hillside. Kenna chuckled. That plucky old woman was her dear Aunt Flora.

The woman rounded the corner and Kenna brought her hand to her mouth in glee. 'Auntie Flora!' she called. Her aunt froze. She looked nearly the same, although a bit fuller in figure than before, having rounded out in the middle.

Her aunt gave a hearty belly laugh before opening her arms wide to Kenna. She rushed to her and gave her a tight squeeze. 'The last time I saw ye, ye were in braids, my dear. What a beauty ye have become. I am so happy to see ye.'

Kenna blushed. Her aunt had always made her feel as if she mattered, and it seemed that hadn't changed, despite the time that had passed. 'I thought you lived in the north,' Kenna commented. 'Father told me you had moved there to be with your daughter and husband.'

She shook her head. 'Partly true. We had been there, but were driven here several years ago due to disputes within the clan. We even took on my maiden name of Hay again for protection and stayed here with your mother. She helped us survive…for a time. Yer uncle died here, and my daughter…'

She paused. 'She couldn't cope. She is back north, married and with babes. I hope to meet them one day, but I do not get on like I used to. And she will not travel here.'

Her aunt's gaze dropped away and she stared down at her hands. That didn't sound like something her cousin would do, but Kenna hadn't seen her since they'd been very young. She would not pry, as it clearly pained her aunt to speak of it, but Kenna knew there was far more to the story. 'I am sorry you do not see her more often,' she sympathised, clutching her aunt's hand.

'Come, come,' her aunt said, regaining her composure. 'Who is this with ye?' she asked.

'This is Mr Dunbar,' Kenna replied.

'Aye. Yer husband?' her aunt asked.

'Nay, Auntie,' Kenna said with a smile. 'He has been my protector along our travels.'

She balked. 'A protector? Why would ye need one, lass?'

'You forget what it's like outside these walls, Flora,' her mother teased.

'Aye, perhaps, but the lass isn'a telling us all. I can feel it in me bones,' she offered, walking over to the stew to stir it.

'Oh?' her mother asked. 'Then what is it, lass?'

When Kenna faltered, Mr Dunbar stepped forward. 'Mr Hay is dead.'

'Dead?' Kenna's mother repeated. Auntie Flora rushed to her side, wrapping her arm around her back.

'Murdered, actually,' Mr Dunbar added.

Her mother crumpled and her aunt guided her to one of the wooden chairs at the single table in the cottage. Flora sat next to her, also overwhelmed with emotion.

Kenna stood, stunned. Once she recovered, she scowled at Mr Dunbar and rushed to her mother, kneeling before her.

'Is it true?' her mother asked as she clutched Kenna's hands.

'It is,' Kenna said softly. 'He wanted us to come here and get your help.'

She hiccupped. 'Help with what?'

'Honouring his dying wish,' Mr Dunbar replied from behind them.

Her mother let out a small whimper. Kenna wanted to throttle the man. Why was he so kind and sensitive one minute and so obtuse the next?

'I thought leaving him there…leaving you both there…would keep you safe,' she murmured. 'Have they found you? Are you running from them now?' she asked desperately, her breaths uneven and ragged. She began coughing.

'Who? Mother, what are you talking about?' Kenna asked. She glanced at her aunt, who looked away.

Mr Dunbar pulled up a chair and sat opposite them, leaning forward on his knees. Even still, he was an imposing figure, and Kenna's pulse increased when his knee bumped into her elbow.

'Mrs Hay,' he said gently, 'your daughter is safe, as are you. Take deep breaths for me.' Her mother did as he asked, and slowly her breathing returned to normal.

Kenna watched him in awe. There it was again—that cool kindness that she found so compelling and confusing all at once.

'Can you tell me what has upset you?' he asked. 'What has you worried for your daughter's safety?'

Kenna sat watching them both but said nothing. After another minute, her mother stared down at her hands that still held Kenna's. She rubbed her thumbs over Kenna's. The movement soothed them both.

After another minute of calm, her mother looked up and nodded. 'It is complicated, and I tried so hard not to involve you. We both did.'

'You mean Father?' Kenna asked.

'Aye.'

'It was your husband who made us promise to come here. He gave us maps and letters,' Mr Dunbar told her. 'Show her,' he said to Kenna. He did not mention the bound book. Perhaps he was forcing her to reveal it, knowing she could not keep it from her mother. She tugged all the items from her coat pocket and met his gaze with resignation.

He responded to her look with a raised brow. There was also a hint of a smirk.

Well played, Mr Dunbar.

She set aside the map but gave the letters and book to her mother. Dierdre Hay stared and drank in the sight of them, especially the book. 'I have not seen this in so long.' Her hand slid over the leather cover with reverence and longing, staring at it as one might look at something deemed lost for ever but then found. It was like how Kenna now looked at her mother, almost as if she had not existed, and now found it hard to believe she was real and alive, sitting before her.

Her mother rested the book gently on the wooden table next to the map and letters. 'All of these things…' she said. 'I should have burned them. All they do is bring harm.' A tear slid down her cheek. 'Bartholomew,' she murmured.

Aunt Flora rubbed her shoulder, and her mother kissed her sister-in-law's cheek. 'I am sorry, Flora. I thought he would be safe.'

'I know, I know,' her aunt murmured. 'No one blames ye.' She wiped a tear from her eye. She and Kenna's father had always had a close sibling relationship, and her sadness at her brother's death was apparent.

'What do you think happened to him, Mrs Hay?' Mr Dunbar asked. 'What is here that is worth killing over?'

His confusion matched Kenna's own. Maps drawn by her father, a packet of old love letters, and a book full of what looked to be personal notes and etchings from a rune caster: why would anyone want these things? How did they fit together at all?

'We didn't even know what it was when we found it,' she said, a wistful look in her eyes. 'Before we had you,' she said, looking at Kenna, 'your father and I would go on our own adventures exploring the woods, caves or whatever suited us, just like when I used to take you.

'When you were younger, we left you with Bridget one day to celebrate the day of our wedding. We found this in a mound far north from here in the Highlands, and we should have left it—it was not ours to take. Whoever had left it hidden there must have known what damage would come from it being unearthed, but we were so intrigued. We wanted to decipher it all, so we took it.

'It took us almost a year to decipher its pages. Then, once I knew what we'd found, I travelled back to the mound to try to put it back, but I couldn't. Soldiers were swarming the mound and digging in and around it: MacDonald soldiers. I rushed home, but we were fearful they had spotted me and might suspect we had the book that verified the messages etched into the mound walls, so we buried it for a time. Then, we decided to separate what we had found and I came to hide here. We knew if they had this the clans in the north would be turned upside down, and with everything so fragile we did all we knew to do to keep it secret.'

'You separated and hid, sacrificing your family in the process,' Mr Dunbar finished.

Kenna couldn't breathe. It felt as she had when she'd been little and had fallen on her back so hard that, for a moment, she hadn't been able to breathe at all. She'd thought she was dying, just as now.

After a minute, she could finally speak. 'Why not just give these MacDonalds what they wanted? You did not owe them anything. What could have been that important that you would leave us, pretend to be dead?' Kenna asked, her voice cracking, and her hands shook.

'We did it to protect you…and the Highlands.' Her mother hesitated. 'These men were brutal… are brutal. I did not want that life for you or anyone in the Highlands.'

'Protect me?' Kenna cried. 'I grieved you and you weren't even dead. Father died because of this. You didn't protect me, Mother.' Kenna had to escape the tiny kitchen in this cottage. She had to be anywhere but here. She rose and started for the door. 'You didn't protect anyone.'

Mr Dunbar pressed a hand to her shoulder but she violently shook it off, as she had at the market square the night of her father's death. 'Leave me be,' she bit out, glaring at him. It didn't matter if he was trying to stop her or console her. It didn't matter that it wasn't his fault. She was angry; she needed to be angry with someone, and he would do very well.

Chapter Seven

Rolf knelt with Mrs Hay, who coughed and sputtered, struggling for breath, and held her hand. Her sister-in-law rushed over with a damp cloth and held it to Mrs Hay's mouth. Light-pink blood coated the rag as she coughed, and part of Rolf folded in. The poor woman didn't have long, if what he knew of such a sickness was true, and her daughter had fled, angry about the past and the present. She was angry about it all, which Rolf understood. But he still felt pained to see the old woman suffer.

If he'd had such few last days or moments with his mother, he would have seized them, no matter how gruesome or painful they might have been. At least she wouldn't have died alone.

Alone. Rolf's chest tightened and the old, familiar rage burned in his chest—rage at his father, rage at the MacDonalds, rage at the unknown. He was weary of being so angry and desperate to discover the truth and set things right. But this woman could help him do that. Selfishly, Rolf needed to keep her alive to get those answers.

He squeezed her hand. 'Try not to struggle so,' he said, remembering how it made every death worse. It mattered not if it was man or beast: life was still life, and death still death. While he didn't know how long this woman had, he wanted her to be comfortable. She also needed her daughter and, as much as Miss Hay didn't want to admit it, she needed her mother. Otherwise, she wouldn't have been so angered by the truth. 'I will bring her back,' he promised the women.

And he would. Even if he had to drag her in by the tattered sleeve of her father's too-large coat.

He commanded himself to take some breaths to counter the desperation he felt. This entire situation was out of his control, and he loathed it. All he wanted was answers, but he was weary, tired and hungry, and now he had to cajole Miss Hay to come back in and see her dying mother. Otherwise, they would glean no further answers at all, and Miss Hay would have to live this moment over and over and have a lifetime of regrets. He wouldn't wish that on anyone, not even an enemy.

And Miss Hay was no enemy, far from it. He was becoming fonder of the little oddities that made her who she was with each hour they spent together. He knew he had just seen the surface of her and, despite the warning bells trying to shy him off, he was becoming more and more entranced by her beauty and strength and wanted to know more about who Kenna Hay truly was. She held secrets too, and he wanted to know what they were—all of them.

He exited the cottage, and the stark contrast of the cold outside from the warmth inside hit him. He shivered as a soft snowfall curled around him and wandered along the worn trail from the cottage and stood, listening.

It wasn't hard to find her. The sound of her soft weeping carried across the air like the tinkle of wind chimes, and he followed the delicate rise and fall of her sorrow. She had tucked herself into the base of an old tree, the stump intact enough to sit on, covered in a light dusting of snow.

'You are wasting your breath,' she muttered as he reached her side. 'I cannot see her. I am too angry.' She hiccupped. 'And I do not wish to say something that hurts her.'

'You may not have a choice,' he said, settling down on the stump on one thigh, so he could sit next to her. His thigh pressed against hers and awareness pierced through him, but he didn't pull away. Instead, he savoured the hiss of desire as it lanced through his core. He stretched out the other leg to balance himself. He focused on the task at hand. 'She is very sick,' he said quietly. There was no way to soften the blow, so he just said it quickly. 'I do not know how much time she has left.'

Fresh tears threatened and she pounded her thigh, the impact of it resonating through his own. 'Why can I not even be allowed the time to be angry? To grieve? Why must I do them all at once?'

'I do not know,' he murmured quietly. How many times had he asked himself that same question and never heard an answer? Far too many to count. 'But you can hit me, if it helps,' he said with a smirk.

She scoffed and narrowed her gaze at him. 'Can I?'

'Aye. It helps my sisters. Perhaps it would help you,' he said with a shrug.

Her eyes widened, flashing a brilliant green-blue, and then she punched him in the arm—hard.

Caught off guard, he almost toppled off the tree

stump, but braced himself with his other leg just in time. 'Ow!' He grimaced and rubbed his shoulder. 'Maybe I shouldn't have offered,' he mumbled.

'Thank you,' she said with a sniff, before wiping her eyes and then standing. 'That truly helped.'

'Glad to be of service,' he said, standing while still rubbing his sore arm.

'You are an odd type of protector, Mr Dunbar—unexpected. And usually people don't surprise me much at all.' With that, she turned and headed back to the cottage, leaving him standing there like a dolt.

'And you, Miss Hay, are full of surprises—which I quite like,' he muttered to himself, rubbing his sore arm. He lagged to allow her mother and her a moment together before following her back inside. When he crossed the threshold of the cottage, all three women were talking excitedly.

'Mr Dunbar, what has happened to my daughter?' the older woman asked. The censure in her voice reminded him of his father. He looked in the woman's direction and saw that she and her sister-in-law were inspecting Miss Hay's temple, which had been hidden by her plaid bandage wrap and woollen cap. Now that she'd removed it, the bandage was obvious, and so was her injury.

'We were attacked,' he replied. 'But—'

'But we are well,' Miss Hay cut in, her eyes pleading with his. 'No need to worry.' She batted her mother's hand away. 'It just needs to be cleaned and re-bandaged, but we must talk first.' She sat down in a chair across from her mother now, creating some distance between them.

'Then we will talk as we eat,' Flora Hay said. 'The stew is ready, and I know you are hungry.'

Rolf couldn't help but smile. 'Aye. We are grateful for a hot meal, thank you.'

'Well, sit down, then,' the older woman fussed, gesturing to the kitchen table. 'And we've fresh bread too.'

He settled in the chair next to Miss Hay, and he noted how she held the satchel in her palm under the table, turning its contents. When she noticed the direction of his interest, she ceased and smoothed the rumpled coat and shirt she wore.

His mouth watered at the savoury smell of the stew, a mixture of meat and potatoes, when it was set down before him. The feel of the steam on his face soothed him, as did the safety of this place, a cosy cottage in a village far removed from the current disputes of the clans and the British threat. He had achieved the first part of his goal: they had reached the Lost Village, found Dierdre Hay, and his charge, Miss Hay, was still alive.

The topics as they ate were light fare, and Rolf enjoyed hearing stories of Miss Hay as a child, a precocious and imaginative little girl with lopsided braids. Despite her protests, he could see that she loved hearing those stories too, and being with two women she loved dearly and had been without for far too long. It reminded him of how much he missed his siblings and their families, and how essential his mission was to keep them safe.

After the table had been cleared and the dishes washed and tidied, they started to settle in for the more serious discussion about their travels and their reasons for being there.

'I know we have much to discuss, but perhaps you'd like a chance to clean up and change—especially you,' Mrs Hay said, eyeing her daughter, still dressed in worn and dirty men's clothes that hung off her body like a discarded grain sack.

Miss Hay looked at him. 'Aye. Could we, Mr Dunbar? I promise not to take too long.'

'Of course,' he answered, also eager to wipe off the remains of such a difficult day, despite how much he wanted to discuss what information she had.

As had been suggested on their arrival, Rolf travelled over to Doran Adair's cottage for a quick wash and to borrow a change of clothes until his own could be washed and mended. The snowfall was heavier, but the cottage wasn't far, and he knocked loudly on the man's door. Doran opened it quickly, as if he had been expecting Rolf. He nodded a greeting and allowed Rolf inside.

The leader of the village lived a humble and orderly life. His cottage was pristine and utilitarian with each possession serving a purpose, except for one set of items that caught Rolf's attention: a small stack of leather-bound books by the man's bed. Rolf couldn't help but smile.

'My one vice,' Doran said, following Rolf's gaze. 'I find it is one of the few things that help me sleep. Escaping into those pages has given me much peace.'

Rolf nodded. 'Soldier?'

'Aye. As were you,' he said. It was a statement, rather than a question, and one that Rolf couldn't refute.

'I envy you. I am still searching for what shall bring me peace,' Rolf replied, and he was. 'I am trying blacksmithing now.'

'And?' he asked.

Rolf shrugged. 'I doubt I will have the patience for it, but I will try a bit longer.'

'Good luck,' Doran replied. 'And you will find what it is that brings you peace.'

'I hope you are right.'

'I am never wrong, so you can count on it.' Doran handed him a pile of clothes that had already been set out. 'You can change in my room. I put a basin of water in there as well with a cloth to wash up.'

'Thank you.' Rolf accepted the clothes, walked into the room, closed the door and began to strip. He dipped the cloth in the water and wiped his face. He winced as the water hit some of the fresh cuts and bruises from the day's adventures.

'So, how did you meet Miss Hay?' Doran asked on the other side of the door.

Rolf smirked and shook his head. He couldn't blame the man for his questions. Rolf would have done the same. He was a stranger, after all.

'Through her father, who owned an antique shop in Melrose,' he replied, trying to be as honest but vague as possible. This man would know a lie.

'Melrose?'

'Aye. He paid me to bring her here safely after he was wounded.'

'Wounded?' Doran asked.

'In the marketplace. Whoever did it was skilled,' Rolf said, wincing as he removed a piece of plaid that was sticking to his burned forearm. 'It was a quick mortal wound—single cut to the gut.'

Doran cursed. 'Why?'

'I wish I knew,' he replied. 'We are hoping to find answers here, now that Miss Hay is reunited with her mother and aunt.'

Rolf finished wiping himself off and began shrugging on the borrowed trews, tunic and coat. All of them fitted as if they were his own. He and Doran were a close match in many ways.

He emerged from the room and Doran nodded to him. 'I thought they would fit. Care for a tonic before you return to the cottage?' he offered. 'I'm having one myself.'

Rolf hesitated.

'It may lessen some of the ache. I drink one after I have had such…battles.'

Rolf's body was aching, and the pain was throbbing through him now that the rush of trying to survive had drained out of him. He nodded and accepted a tankard from Doran. It was a soothing chamomile with mint and something else he couldn't quite name, but it seemed familiar somehow.

They drank in the quiet silence that he'd come to appreciate from when he'd been a soldier. When he'd nearly reached the bottom of his cup, he felt warm and relaxed, so much so that he struggled to keep his eyes open. They fluttered closed once and then again.

'Apologies. I can't seem to stay awake,' he muttered, trying to force his eyes to remain open. His fingers tingled. Something wasn't right. A dull warning throbbed in his brain.

Doran set the tankard on the table next to him and rose from his chair. 'Do not fight it, my brother,' he said. 'This is exactly what was supposed to happen.'

Before Doran reached Rolf, the world went dark and silent.

Rolf woke foggily, but once the world came into view and he didn't recognise it he shot up from the chair he was in. The metal tankard on his lap clattered to the wooden floor.

'Ah, you are awake at last,' Doran said, walking into the room from his bedroom.

Rolf stared at the empty tankard on the ground and glared at Doran as he stitched together what had happened. The only way he could have slept that long and that deeply was with a laced tonic.

'Why did you drug me?' Rolf demanded. 'And what have you done with Miss Hay?' He had stood too quickly, and it made him sway. He placed a bracing hand on the chair and then collapsed back into it, squeezing his eyes shut until the dizziness passed.

'Apologies on the dosage. Afraid I made it a bit too strong, but I wanted to be sure you were out.' Doran sat back in the chair opposite him and shrugged. 'And do not worry about Miss Hay. She is well, with her mother and aunt. No doubt she is probably sleeping, as you were.'

'You drugged her too?'

Doran shrugged. 'Perhaps.'

Now he was angry. 'Why?'

'Safety. We do not have many visitors here and we maintain our safety and privacy by being careful about those we do have.'

Rolf waited for more. He knew there had to be more.

'For instance,' he said. 'I now know you are not who you say you are, *Mr Dunbar.*' He narrowed his gaze at him. 'Time for you to tell me the truth. You will not see Miss Hay ever again if you don't.'

Now he was furious. 'Do *not* dare hurt her.'

Doran balked, insulted by Rolf's accusation. 'Nay, I would never hurt her, but *you*? I would have no problem with that. You are a liar.'

Rolf said nothing.

'So, what are your intentions? I know you are not a Dunbar, as you claim,' he said, removing a ring from the table and making a show of analysing it before returning it. 'I found this in your belongings. A Cameron crest, I believe?'

Rolf stiffened.

'Based on how the colour drained from your face, Miss Hay does not know your identity either. But why? Why pretend to be her protector and aid her on this journey as someone else? Hell, you look as if you were almost killed. You are covered in bruises and cuts.'

Doran settled back in his chair. Although he might have looked relaxed to another man, Rolf could see the man was livid and ready to attack at a moment's notice. The long scar along his cheek whitened from the flush of blood to his face.

Rolf needed to choose his next words carefully. He sat in silence and held Doran's glare. Unable to think of any path that would gain the man's trust other than the truth, Rolf sighed and let his head rest on the back of the chair. How much of the truth did he dare share? He was still so far from achieving his mission, and his family was counting on him.

So was Miss Hay.

The woman would hate him once she knew of his deception, and what would keep this man from telling her? His plan was crumbling quickly. He lifted his head. 'Aye, I am a Cameron. I am the second son, and my brother is laird.'

Doran nodded. 'Why the deception?'

'Miss Hay would not have accepted my protection if she knew who I was.'

'Why not?'

'Because my family may be part of the reason why her father was killed.'

Doran's brow lifted. 'I expected many reasons, but not that one. So, you are protecting her out of duty or honour to make up for what happened to her father.' He leaned forward and rested his elbows on his knees.

'In a sense. I found him wounded on the street and he made me promise to protect her. I was meant to meet him for information. I was late, and he ended up dead because of it.'

Doran whistled. 'And when Miss Hay discovers this?'

'I haven't planned that far. And I am hopeful you will keep this between us until I find a way to tell her the truth. Otherwise, she will flee and try to travel to Loch's End alone.'

'Why? Why has she travelled this far at all?'

'Her father made her promise to deliver what she has to the family herself.'

'Why not just tell her the truth and take whatever she has back to Loch's End yourself and spare her the danger and upset of the journey? Send her back to Melrose, or she can stay here with us and be safe.'

Rolf chuckled. 'You do not know her well, but I am starting to. She will not just let this go. She is determined to see this through, no matter the danger.'

Rolf wasn't ready to let her go either—not yet. *Perhaps never.* The thought unnerved him. Where had that come from? They were no match, even if he wanted that to be so. Even if somehow he dared risk grasping for that sort of happiness, once she knew he was a Cameron she would be gone. His hope for them was attached to a withering vine.

'Why should I keep it a secret? What is so important about this mission of yours?'

'To be honest, I am not even sure myself yet. I came looking for information on my parents, and Bartholomew Hay had letters to share with me from my mother. The maps, letters and book Miss Hay found hidden in her home by her father seem to somehow be linked, but I do not know how, and Mrs Hay was just beginning to enlighten us about it when her daughter and I were separated and drugged.'

'I do not believe she was drugged,' Doran offered. 'Just you.' He smiled.

Rolf shook his head. 'The point is we are losing time to work it all out, and from what I could tell Mrs Hay is quite ill.'

Doran looked down and then up with a nod. 'Aye. She is.'

'So?' Rolf asked. 'What say you? Will you keep my secret or not?'

'On one condition.'

Rolf waited, knowing full well the man's one condition would require a large concession, whatever it was, and that he probably wouldn't like it one bit.

'I have business this morn, but I will join you when Mrs Hay relays the import of the items from her husband. I will know what threat you have brought upon us. I need to know how to protect my people.'

'Threat?' Rolf asked.

'Aye. I have met Camerons before and there is always more at play than first meets the eye.'

Rolf would have objected, but the man was right. It was always complicated to be a Cameron. Today in the Lost Village would be no different.

'Correct me if I'm wrong, but based on the look upon your face I would venture you don't even know the extent of the dilemma you are in, which makes me all the more concerned,' Doran said.

Unable to utter a lie, Rolf sat silently, and Doran cursed under his breath. 'Exactly as I thought,' he muttered before he rose to leave. 'Camerons are all the same.'

Chapter Eight

Kenna's blurry world came into focus, and she yawned. Even though she didn't even know how she'd ended up on the settee, swathed in a cocoon of blankets, she didn't mind. She felt warm, luxurious and as though she had slept for days.

'Glad ye decided to join us,' Aunt Flora said with a chuckle as she darned clothes by the fire. The woman seemed to be mending the hem of a gown. Kenna scanned the room, and saw her mother wasn't there. Her pulse increased as she surveyed the room again.

'Yer mother is at the market, lass. Ye need not worry. She wanted to make yer favourite supper this eve, especially since ye slept straight through any morning meals,' Aunt Flora replied to Kenna's unspoken question.

'What happened? I cannot remember anything after getting washed and changed. I came in here, sat down on the settee and...'

'Ye fell right asleep. Didn't even hear Mr Adair come by to let us know Mr Dunbar would be staying with him for the night. Evidently, the man was just as exhausted.'

While surprised by the news that Mr Dunbar hadn't even attempted to return to question her mother, Kenna didn't balk at the gift of time she'd had with her aunt and the brief reprieve she'd had from him. They had spent a great deal of time together, and she was becoming a bit more attached to him than she'd like to admit. He would be leaving her after this mission of theirs was complete. The idea of him leaving her for good made her stomach flip.

It was best not to think of anything of the sort. She shook her head to shake off the feeling that came with it, a feeling she didn't wish to name. It was ridiculous to miss a man such as him; most of the time he was downright difficult. At other times, he was so kind and handsome, she could scarcely stand it.

Kenna yawned again and tried to sit up, but every muscle in her body protested, making the memories of yesterday's attacks more vivid. She closed her eyes and winced as she forced herself to push through the pain to sit up. Her head pounded.

'No need to force yourself, my dear. I couldn't help but notice ye had several bruises from the attack ye sustained.' She tsked. 'I hate to think what poor Mr Dunbar looked like.' She smiled. 'Although, he isn't so hard to set one's eyes upon, is he?' she teased and winked at her.

Kenna couldn't help but laugh. 'Nay, he isn't,' she replied. 'And he seems kind, although at times he can be rather difficult and disagreeable.' She repositioned the blankets around herself and settled back against the cushions. Her fingertips tingled at the memory of the night before when he'd sat beside her consoling her, his leg touching hers.

And then she'd punched him in the arm. She cringed. Why had she done that?

'Most men are, dear,' Aunt Flora replied.

Kenna had lost the thread of their conversation, consumed by her own thoughts. 'Apologies, Auntie, I cannot keep up this morn. What did you say?'

'I was merely saying most men are kind but a wee bit difficult and disagreeable at times. Just like yer Mr Dunbar.' She lifted her brow for effect and then went back to mending.

Kenna chuckled. 'Even Uncle?'

'Aye,' Aunt Flora replied with a wistful look in her eyes. 'But I loved him fiercely anyway.'

'How did you all end up here at the Lost Village?' Kenna asked, fiddling with the edge of one of the blankets.

Flora set aside her mending in her lap. 'We came here with our daughter to hide after the unrest about a decade ago now. We knew yer mother was here, and we were so very happy for a while. Then, when yer uncle got sick and died, it became too painful for our daughter to stay. Too many memories, she said, even though the memories of him and us as a family is exactly *why* I stay. She lives with her family on Skye.'

'I hardly remember her. I cannot even remember her name,' Kenna commented, leaning forward.

'No worries, my dear, ye were so young. Her name is Nora. From what I can tell, ye two have much in common: headstrong, smart and determined to forge ahead when ye set yer mind to something.'

'I hope to see her again some day,' Kenna said. 'I have never been to Skye.'

'Nor I. I hope that they come back and surprise me with a visit soon, so I can meet my grandchildren,' she said wistfully.

Kenna smiled. 'That would be wonderful.'

'Aye.'

They fell into silence.

Kenna bit her lip. Would she be a mother one day? Such thoughts seemed so far away and in some other future world outside of what she dared even hope for. Her world was upside down, and after yesterday's attacks she did not even know if she could count on tomorrow, let alone hope for a future life and family of her own.

'Why don't ye get up and ready for what remains of the day, lass? Ye can complete yer ablutions and try on the gown yer mother put on the bed for ye in the room there. See if it fits ye. I am working on pulling out the hems of a few more that we hope might fit.'

Kenna rose, grateful to escape her own thoughts and worries about the future. Focusing on the present was essential. Getting too caught up in thoughts of what her life would be like after she returned home to Melrose all alone would do her no good. She kissed her Aunt Flora and hustled into the bedroom, eager to shake off her melancholy and dress.

The cosy bedroom was well cared for, and small. Carved figurines, a singular painting and colourful quilts made the room cheerful and warm, just as she remembered her mother before she had left them. She lifted one of the quilts to her nose and smiled. It even smelled like her: a mixture of lavender and sage. Kenna's eyes watered and she fought the wave of emotion threatening. Why had she missed so many years with her mother only to find her now when she was so ill? Why had any of the horrible things of the past week happened? As usual, there was no answer.

Kenna completed her ablutions and stripped down to her underclothes. She slid a grey dress over her head. It was a little snug, but she didn't mind. In the few days she had worn her father's clothes, she had grown weary of the extra weight and material hanging off her body. She smoothed the dress over her waist, enjoying feeling like a woman again.

Spying a looking glass and comb, she brushed through her hair and braided it back into a simple, smooth plait. While she had bruises and marks from her injuries, it was a vast improvement to be wearing clean clothes and to have her hair combed. She felt along her waist and balked. Where were her runes? And how had she not noted their absence until now? She rushed from the room just as someone knocked on the door.

'Auntie,' she called, 'have you seen my...?'

Aunt Flora made it to the door before Kenna could complete her question.

'Good morn, Mrs Hay.'

At the sound of Mr Dunbar's voice, Kenna swallowed the rest of her question. It would have to wait.

'And to ye, Mr Dunbar, although it is more like afternoon,' Aunt Flora teased, letting him in.

He had to stoop slightly to enter, which Kenna hadn't noticed yesterday. He wore a clean tunic, a dark-grey coat and matching trews which fitted him...quite well. So well that she could see muscles flexing beneath the material covering his thighs and shoulders, something she had not noticed the day before. He looked almost naked without the large green and red plaid he'd worn over his clothes. His dark hair flopped a bit over his eyes, and his face was clean and freshly shaved. When she met his gaze, a fluttering of awareness filled her stomach, and she gripped her hands together in front of her waist.

Saints be. How was he becoming more handsome with each passing day? But there he was, walking towards her, assessing her as he did so. His gaze travelled along her from head to toe and lingered along the wound at her temple and the scratches on her cheekbone and bruised chin.

'Did you sleep well, Miss Hay?' His blue eyes were warm, concerned and searching.

'Aye. And you, Mr Dunbar?' she asked, wanting to know if he was well.

How odd. What was wrong with her? She felt awkward and a bit shy after having time apart from him.

Ack. She had missed him. Perhaps her head wound had affected her more than she'd first thought. How could she miss a man who'd been vexing her so only yesterday evening?

'Perhaps too well,' he answered. 'I slept far later this morn than I planned and have delayed our talk with your mother.'

'She is out anyhow. I just woke myself.'

'I may be able to help ye,' Aunt Flora said. 'There is much yer mother and I have discussed during our years together here. Come, sit.'

She gestured and they came and joined her in the small sitting area before the hearth. The settee that had been so comfortable and cosy now felt rather cramped with Mr Dunbar next to her. She edged closer to the arm of it to try to gain some space between them, but it was no use. They were still touching, and the feel of his thigh against hers threatened to drive her mad. But the more space she allowed, the more space he seemed to swallow up. If she wasn't careful, she'd be on the floor.

He seemed oblivious to it all as he chatted with her aunt about the weather, pending snow and the best way to track a lost cow. Kenna felt like an outsider looking in at them, and her mind seemed unable to catch up with their discussion, or perhaps it was how surreal it was. Did it matter what the weather would be when they'd been attacked the day before and her mother was dying? She sat quietly wondering whether her promise to her father was so important to sacrifice themselves over, when her mother came in, her hands full of wrapped goods from the market.

'Glad to see everyone is up and together!' she called, setting the items on the table.

'You must have quite a bustling market here, Mother. The village seemed quite small when we came in.'

'Nay, dear. You have seen the smallest portion of it. If you continue, it widens out to a most impressive centre where we have a weekly market to swap and barter goods. You were lucky it happened to be today, so I could get all your favourites.' She winked at her as she unpacked meat and vegetables. 'And, once we eat this eve, we shall have a rune-casting so I may see how your skills have grown.'

Kenna stilled. She didn't have to turn to feel the intensity of Mr Dunbar's stare. 'Runes?' he asked. 'I do not understand.'

Her mother cocked her head. 'Has she not spoken to you of her gift, Mr Dunbar?'

'Nay,' he replied. 'What does she speak of, Miss Hay? What gift is it that you possess and do not tell me of?' he asked, touching his hand gently to her forearm.

Kenna sighed, squared her shoulders and plucked up the courage to face him. To her surprise, he seemed interested rather than full of condemnation, but perhaps that was because he didn't yet know what gifts she hid from him.

Uncertainty made her palms sweat. She smoothed her hands along her thighs and began. 'You know the pouch that I have worn along my waist? I know you noticed it as I caught you watching me turn the runes within them several times over the last few days.'

'Aye.' He turned slightly to face her. 'I did notice. Each time I saw you doing so, you stopped and tried to hide them from me. And you do not wear them now,' he said, pointing to her waist, where its brooch and sack of runes were absent.

Her mother blushed and rushed over to Kenna. She removed a pouch from her gown pocket. 'I bought you a new pouch for them, my dear. I noticed your other was quite worn and, well, a bit bloody from your travels.'

At first, Kenna felt defensive and angry at her mother for getting rid of her old satchel, but when she held the new pouch in her palm she was moved by the gesture. It was a dark emerald-green and smooth, like silk. And seemed expensive. 'You should not have, Mother, but I love it. It is beautiful.'

Kenna held the pouch in her hands and turned the runes within it. The familiar peace that came with having the weight of them shifting in her hands settled upon her. All was well. All was well.

'What are they?' Mr Dunbar asked, breaking into her reverie. 'I do not believe I even know what they are.'

Kenna pulled the fine drawstrings out and opened it. The small, polished stones caught the light of the room, and she could see their many symbols. She smiled. They were like old friends to her.

'We will answer all of your questions about them, but first…' she paused and leaned the pouch over to him '…take one,' she offered.

'Which one?' he asked.

'Whichever one speaks to you. There is no wrong choice.'

He hesitated. 'Go on,' she encouraged. 'You can even spread them out on the table there if you wish, or merely look through them in the pouch.' She handed him the bag.

This was her favourite part of introducing someone to runes: watching the wonder and confusion mix with an intense desire to know more than one ever could at this stage. For quiet minutes, Mr Dunbar looked through the runes and studied them as the fire crackled in the background. The way he looked at them with such interest and turned them over with gentle care in his fingers intrigued her. He was not dismissive but curious, and when he settled on one his features softened.

'I have seen this one before,' he said.

'May I see it?' Kenna asked with a jump in her pulse.

Seeing which rune spoke to a person was the first link to understanding the essence of who they were. When she saw the single stone with what she always viewed as butterfly wings, she couldn't help but smile. Her mother and aunt did the same.

He looked around at all of them. 'What is it?' he asked.

'That is Dagaz. It means "daylight" or "dawn",' Kenna said as he turned it over in his fingertips.

'It often hints at illumination, transformation and hope,' her mother said, sitting on the arm of the settee near Kenna. Dierdre ran her hand over Kenna's plait as she had when she'd been a girl. It soothed her to the core.

'Is that what ye seek, Mr Dunbar?' her aunt asked.

He looked up from the rune, although he did not cease running his thumb over the butterfly symbol. 'Aye, Mrs Hay. More than you will ever know.'

Chapter Nine

Rolf could scarcely breathe. How did they know what he wanted, truly wanted, down to the marrow of his bones? How did this small stone know? Rolf rubbed it between his fingers, as he would a worry stone, and felt a peace he had not felt in some time. Or perhaps it was not the stone, but being here with these women, or just Miss Hay.

Kenna.

How he longed to call her that, but he dared not broach such intimacies until she wished it, and she did not wish it yet. He could tell by how she'd tried to ease away from him on the settee and how she wouldn't hold his gaze for long. He could not rush such a thing, nor did he know if he should. The woman deserved the best of men, which wasn't him at this point in time. He was too consumed by the past, his family's secrets and all the lies he had told her.

She didn't even know his real name. But perhaps this…this tiny stone…could be the beginning of the truth.

'Why did you pick this one?' Miss Hay asked. Her lips were parted, and she looked almost breathless for his answer—as if his answer would move them forward. And maybe it would if he told her all that had come to him when he'd seen that symbol and felt the cool weight of it in his hand.

He held her sea-green gaze. 'I have seen it before.'

'Where?' she asked.

He shook his head. 'I do not know if you will believe me,' he said.

He itched to look at his ankle, but feared he was wrong. He would look a fool if he was, but how many times had he traced his finger over the scar upon his ankle? He knew the symbol. He had just never known what it meant or why he had it… until now.

Miss Hay placed her hand on his forearm. 'Where?' she asked.

Gooseflesh skittered along his skin, and his throat dried in anticipation of what was next. He bent down and tugged up the bottom of his trews to reveal the shilling-sized raised scar he'd had on his ankle for as long as he could remember.

'May I?' she asked.

He nodded and she leaned closer, her long plait sliding along his arm as she moved; the scent of rose and peony was a reminder of her proximity. She touched the pad of her fingertip to the scar and traced over it, as he had a thousand times before. He sucked in a breath and almost shivered from the intimate feel of the contact, and from knowing finally what the symbol meant.

'This has been carved. Did you do this?' she asked.

'Nay,' he replied. 'But I have had it as long as I can remember, and none of my siblings know how I got it. They said I just had a bandage over it one day when I was young.'

'Did your parents never tell you how it happened?'

'They claimed not to know,' he replied, shifting on the settee. 'But they were good at keeping secrets.' As soon as he said the words, it felt like a betrayal, and he wished he could gather them back.

'We all have secrets,' Doran Adair said from behind them. Rolf balked and covered his ankle before sitting back up.

Doran met Rolf's gaze with a fierce intensity he didn't like, but Rolf knew why. He had left the cottage without the man, despite the agreement they had made, but Rolf had been too eager to see the Hays to wait for the man to return from his outing.

'Aye, we do,' Rolf replied, letting Doran know he understood the threat.

'We were just beginning to show Mr Dunbar the runes,' Flora Hay explained. 'Seems he may have been acquainted with the power of the runes and not even known it.' She gestured to his ankle.

Rolf hesitated. What did he have to lose? He lifted the leg of his trews again in the hope that showing his scar to Doran would soften some of the man's anger. To his surprise, it worked. Doran settled into the last empty seat in the room, a lone chair by the hearth near Flora Hay.

'So, what are runes?' Rolf asked, to shift the focus from his ankle. He covered the scar and sat back up, turning his full attention to Miss Hay.

'Perhaps it is easiest to start from what they are not.'

'Meaning?'

'Have you heard of them before?' Kenna's mother asked.

'Honestly? Only in regard to witchcraft and devilry...' He paused. 'And a few folk tales that I think were merely meant to keep me and my brother out of trouble, but I have never understood what they were.' He chuckled.

'That is how most people view them before they experience them,' Flora Hay muttered, setting her work aside on the table. She shook her head and mumbled something that sounded like a curse under her breath.

'Sister,' Dierdre Hay said, trying to smother a smirk.

'What I think my aunt is saying is the runes are a tool of intuition rather than devilry. Right, Auntie?' Miss Hay lifted her brow at her aunt.

'Nay. That isn't what I meant. I tire of all this negative talk of runes when they are nothing of the sort,' Flora Hay asserted.

'She is right,' Doran added. 'I was once like you, Mr Dunbar. I was a soldier who didn't believe in such things as intuition and guidance by mere stones, but I am a believer now. You will see.'

'Truly?' Rolf asked, unable to keep the utter surprise from his voice. 'I would not have thought a leader such as yourself would admit such.'

'You will see for yourself,' he added. 'Just as I did. I can hardly wait.' He leaned back in his chair and crossed his arms against his chest with a satisfied smile.

Rolf frowned as a ripple of unease settled on his bones. 'And how do I see for myself?' he asked.

'Come, let us gather at the table so you can see them all spread out and we can explain how they work,' Miss Hay suggested. Her eyes were bright and her tone light, as if she was eager to show him a new toy. Perhaps she was.

'Will it help me to understand this?' he asked, pointing to the book Bartholomew Hay had hidden, and most likely died to protect, which sat on the table as they all settled around it.

She paused and looked down at it. Her grip on the back of the chair tightened and her knuckles whitened before she answered. 'Aye,' she replied and then sat down. 'But there is much to explain, and...'

'One thing at a time, Mr Dunbar,' Flora Hay said. 'Sit.'

Anticipation thrummed in him as Miss Hay removed a white cloth tucked in the sleeve of her gown and spread it out on the wooden table. She smoothed it with her palm with the ease of someone who had done such a thousand times. Then, she lifted her pouch of runes, turned it in her hand and spilled the contents of the bag onto the table, the stones scattering along the cloth. She let them settle and then carefully turned them all face up, spreading them out. Her graceful and purposeful movements made him wonder how many times she had done this same thing before.

He studied each one as she turned them over and at first all the symbols overwhelmed him. But as he sat with them, looking over each one and counting how many there were, an unexpected calmness came over him, as if he too had done this before, although he hadn't.

He couldn't have. Could he?

There were twenty-five stones in all, and several symbols made more sense to him than others. Some of the carvings reminded him of trees or birds, and others of mountains or water. One was even blank. There was something soothing about seeing them all out, as if they offered up possibilities all on their own just by being. Perhaps this was what she spoke about and why she found them so soothing.

'Which other ones speak to you?' Miss Hay asked softly. 'Pick three, if you can.'

He looked up and realised they were all watching him. Heat flushed his skin. How long had he just been staring at them, lost in his own thoughts? He shifted in his chair and looked at them again, wondering if there was a right or wrong way to make his selections.

He chose three more runes that gave him comfort and intrigued him. Picking them out without knowing what they meant was like selecting satchels without knowing what was in them, and he felt like a child opening presents on a special day. A twinge of nerves mixed with his excitement. He couldn't help but note the surprise in her eyes as he set them down before her.

'Have you studied that journal?' she asked, her brow furrowing.

'Nay,' he answered. 'I flipped through it, but I didn't know what I was looking at. To be honest, I still don't know what I'm looking at.'

She smiled and seemed relieved. 'You aren't meant to,' she answered simply, as if what she said made all the sense in the world. 'Runes are a mystery.'

'I don't understand,' he said.

'The word "rune" means "mystery",' her mother volunteered. 'Each symbol is believed to hold its own energy and meaning. When you pair the runes with your own intuition, they can help you work out potential solutions or guide your choices.'

'So, are these symbols a solution?' he asked, leaning forward, even more eager to know what the symbols he chose represented.

'You chose them based on what question is first

in your heart. What is your question, Mr Dunbar?' Miss Hay asked.

Her gaze was unflinching and urgent in a way he didn't understand. But he couldn't tell her what was in his heart now, could he? She still didn't know who he was. He balked, uncertain as to what to do.

After a moment, she merely smiled and looked back to the runes. 'No need to tell us. Just hold the question in your mind.' She studied the stones, her face scrunched in concentration. 'I will tell you what the symbols stand for, and you can interpret what solutions they hold for you.'

The fire crackled and Rolf held his breath until she finally began.

'This one,' she said, 'that looks like the top of a tree often stands for protection, healing, self-defence or even willpower. Perhaps you are trying to shelter yourself or someone else.'

He nodded.

'And this one...' she said, turning the next stone. 'You see how it looks a bit like two hands reaching for each other? It is a celebration or turning point. It marks a harvest, in a sense when all of one's hard work has paid off.'

He leaned closer, intrigued by her words and how much they paired with his question.

'The M shape of this last rune means movement, change for the better, trust…and partnership. But this…' She paused and her index finger traced the butterfly-wing pattern of the first rune he'd selected. 'It is the most interesting of them, I think, especially knowing it has been carved on you.'

'Why?' he asked, leaning his arms on the table, eager to hear her next words.

'It often stands for illumination, hope and growth—light to darkness; emergence to clarity. In simple terms, it signals a transformation, much like a butterfly.'

Clarity. Transformation. Illumination.

He would have answers. He would discover the truth. The secrets would be uncovered. He and his family would be able to move on. He smiled, and the smile turned into a laugh, a laugh of relief, excitement and hope for the future. If they had been alone, he might have reached over the table, pulled her to him and kissed her fiercely.

'I have never loved a rune so,' he said.

'You have never even seen them before,' Miss Hay countered with a chuckle.

'Nay. But this butterfly,' he said, clutching the rune in his hand, 'gives me hope.'

'They often do, but they also at times signal

other things.' Her gaze dropped away, and her mother reached across the table to clasp her hand.

'What did the runes warn you of?' her mother asked quietly.

Rolf was spellbound. Had the runes warned her of something? Was she a seer through the medium of these stones? Could they warn her about him, or lead her to the truth?

'This,' she said quietly. She scanned the stones and pointed to one with a carved, slanted H on it. 'This stone called to me on the day father was murdered.'

'Disruption,' Flora Hay murmured.

'Father had not returned for our Hogmanay meal, which you both know is his favourite, and then this stone called to me. Once I saw it, I knew something was wrong.'

That familiar sorrow entered her eyes and she looked away, folding her hands neatly back into her lap, leaving the carved, slanted H on the table.

Disruption... Was he part of that disruption? By coming to Melrose and being late for his meeting with Bartholomew Hay, had Rolf served a role in the disruption in Miss Hay's life and her future? And were the stones truly that accurate?

He studied the four he had selected.

Protection. Turning point. Partnership. Trans-

formation. Those words could mean anything, and his mind spun with all the possibilities. 'How did you know the disruption involved your father?' he asked. 'There are so many things it could have been.'

She shrugged. Her gaze was haunted as she recounted that evening when she'd lost him. 'I cannot say, not truly. I felt a tightness within my chest and an urgency to find him. He was late and I just…knew.'

'She has a gift,' her mother added. 'Not many rune casters are so attuned to the stones.'

'Like a seer?' Rolf asked, unsure of what she meant.

Miss Hay flushed and looked away, not answering his question. Did she think he would shame her or ridicule her gift? He resisted the urge to ask her.

''Tis no matter,' her mother said, noting her daughter's reluctance to answer his question. 'We will speak of it later tonight. I cannot wait to see how you have grown in your skills, my dear.' She squeezed her daughter's hand.

Miss Hay smiled back at her. 'Thank you again for the pouch, Mother. It is beautiful.'

Her mother leaned in, kissed her cheek and murmured something in her ear that brought light into Miss Hay's eyes. Rolf wished he'd said whatever it was. He would love to bring Miss Hay such momentary joy. So far, most of what he had brought her was loss and near death.

Some protector he was. Bartholomew Hay was probably cursing him from beyond. Why had this journey been nothing he had expected or planned for? All he'd wanted and hoped for was a resolution, but now all he had were more questions and complications, the greatest of which was Miss Hay. She was a distraction to his fleeting focus, and he needed to work out how to manage it. Even now her sweet peony and rose scent muddled his thoughts. He watched her gather up her runes as Doran spread out the map on the table. He caught Rolf staring at Miss Hay and frowned. Rolf cleared his throat and dropped his gaze as he shifted in his chair.

Curses. The man missed nothing, and he'd just caught Rolf mooning over the woman like a lad. He needed to regain his focus. He needed to work out how the maps, letters and journal all connected, so he could know how to protect his family from whatever secrets remained. Then, he could travel home to Loch's End and leave all of this behind him, especially his budding infatuation with Kenna Hay.

She'd be far safer without him. It was what was best for everyone.

Liar. Well, it was best for her.

'Do you know anything about this map, Mrs Hay?' Rolf asked. 'I know your daughter said her father made it based on where the compass rose was located, but have you seen it before?'

The old woman ran her palms across the worn parchment, letting her fingers linger longer upon some locations and symbols. She studied it for several minutes, and they waited in silence.

'I remember when he made this map,' she said, her eyes wistful. 'He has added much to it since then,' she continued. 'I think he was still trying to determine what it all meant and how to make things right between the clans in the Highlands.' She shook her head and sighed. 'Bartholomew,' she mumbled. 'I think that was how he got himself killed.'

'What do you mean?' Doran asked.

'I believe he was plotting the real ownership of those lands on this map. We talked often about how the runes hinted at the fact that someone had altered the original borders from those on the walls in the mound.'

Rolf's stomach clenched. 'Altering clan boundaries is a serious accusation.'

'Aye, it is, which is why we tried to keep what we discovered a secret from the MacDonalds. They have the most to lose if all is revealed. I am not sure why he kept at it. Something had to have sparked his interest in this again.' She sat back in her chair and rubbed her eyes.

'You do not have to continue, Mother,' Miss Hay insisted. 'Do not strain yourself. I know you are unwell.'

Her mother smiled. 'This is more alive than I have felt in months. I do not want to miss a moment of it. Perhaps a tonic to dull the ache and then I will be set to rights.'

Her sister-in-law nodded and rose from the table. 'I have just the thing, dear. Give me but a moment to heat some water over the fire.'

While she set to the task of making a tonic, Rolf watched Miss Hay's mother. What could have set her husband on to this task they had agreed to set aside years ago? Had the MacDonalds found them? Was it something related to his mother's letters? It had to relate to him and to Miss Hay's safety.

Kenna.

He studied her as she spoke softly to her mother. It had to be something that threatened *her*. Why else would a father re-engage in something that he and his wife had set aside for the sole purpose of protecting their daughter in the first place?

He asked the only person that might know. 'Miss Hay, had your father's behaviour changed at all over the last few months?'

She ceased talking with her mother and shook her head. 'Nothing I can think of that was odd or unusual. Although this year he had made great gains with the shop. He had saved it and us from ruin.'

'How did he do that?'

'He had taken to travelling through the small surrounding towns at various times of the month and always brought back items to add to the shop, which was something he'd never done before. He'd generally relied on those in Melrose for his inventory and items to sell.' She studied him. 'Why?'

'Did you work in the shop with him?'

'Of course,' she added. 'I could not allow him to attempt to do all of that alone. I enjoyed it, too. Always interesting people coming in and out of the shop and new items to price and display.'

'Had the patrons changed? New customers you had not seen, perhaps?' Doran asked, moving his chair forward.

She shrugged and played with the end of her plait. 'Some. People of finer clothes who were willing to buy more and pay more for items, now that you mention it, but no one stood out. Most men in fancy trews and waistcoats seem the same to me.'

Rolf smiled at that bit. Most likely those men had spotted her beauty, even if she had not noted their interest. Poor sots; she'd never given them any notice, despite their fancy trews.

She ceased toying with the end of her braid. 'Although, now that you mention it, I do remember the day he discovered a batch of letters hidden in the secret compartment of an old wooden puzzle box a man had sold him. I do not know if they are the same as those he had hidden in the clock, but they must be. He was excited about them and then later, when I asked him what was in them, he scoffed. He merely told me they were of no importance and he had thrown them away. I didn't think much of it at the time. Evidently, I should have.' Her shoulders slumped. 'It may have prevented all of this.'

'Nay,' Rolf countered. 'How could you possibly have known? And the man who killed him would have killed you as well if you had stood in his way.'

She shivered and rubbed her arms. *Ack.* Why had he said that? He'd upset her, which was the last thing he wished to do. Doran cut him a glance of annoyance. The man was right: Rolf had made a misstep, but there was no unwinding it.

'And the letters? Can you tell me about them or describe the box? Is it still at the shop?' Doran asked.

Mrs Hay accepted a tankard of steaming tonic from her sister-in-law, who settled back down at the table with them.

Miss Hay hesitated. 'Aye. Father decided to keep the box rather than sell it. Since it was a wooden puzzle box, it intrigued him. He must have stored the letters in it before he moved them to the wall clock. It's all very odd.'

'Have you read those letters since you removed them from the clock? I believe you said they were love letters,' Rolf mentioned, his pulse increasing. He had to know if they were really his mother's.

'Aye,' she said. 'But I stopped. They were rather…' She searched for the right word. 'Intimate. I felt they were not meant for me to read. It was correspondence between lovers.'

'Were there any names or signatures on them?' Rolf asked. Doran shot him a warning glance, but Rolf ignored it. He had waited too long. He could wait no longer to know whether or not the letters Bartholomew Hay had used to lure Rolf here were really from his mother.

He also had to know who the other person was. He hoped and prayed it was his father, but he knew it wouldn't be. His father had been far too cold and calculating to write love letters, especially ones that could be described as 'intimate in nature'.

'We will look. May I see them?' Miss Hay asked.

Her aunt rose and brought them to the table, resting them in front of Kenna, just an arm's length from Rolf. It took all his self-control not to lunge across the table, snap them up and run from the cottage to read them. For days he had waited to read those letters, days. He laced his hands together and gripped them to keep his baser instincts at bay. He hadn't wanted to give away his interest in them, so he had ignored them when she'd first shown them to him. Now, he was salivating at the chance to read their contents.

She pulled the red ribbon that bound them and opened the wax seal of the first letter. She scanned it, flipped to the last of the pages and squinted. 'They are signed "Iso".'

Rolf's body went numb and his fingers tingled. *Iso.*

What he'd hoped for and yet feared was true.

The letters were from his mother, Isolde... known by those who loved her as Iso.

Chapter Ten

Kenna couldn't help but notice how Mr Dunbar's face softened at the mention of a woman named Iso. She pulled a letter from the top of the bunch and skimmed it before jolting to a stop. She re-read the paragraph. Her stomach dropped to the floor and sickness threatened.

'What is it?' Mr Dunbar asked, his brow furrowed. 'You've paled.'

'What is the date on the letter on the bottom of the stack?' she asked him as she flipped to the back side of the letter she held. As she feared, there was nothing more to read.

'The seventeenth of June 1717.'

'And the dates of the others?' she asked, her pulse increasing. 'Look at them all. What is the latest date?'

'Why?' he asked. 'What is wrong?'

'I must know if this is the last letter in their exchange. I thought this was the first of the bunch, but it may be the last.' Her voice shook and the letter trembled in her hand. She set it on the table and commanded herself to breathe.

Doran grabbed the bunch of letters and divided it up, handing each person a small stack so the contents could be analysed quickly. Kenna waited. Her heart skipped and clattered in her chest. She was eager to consult her runes, but part of her deep down knew the answer to her question: she was holding the last letter this woman named Iso had ever written.

'This part is from a year later, in 1718,' Doran offered before setting them down.

'More from 1717,' her aunt replied.

'Aye,' her mother answered. '1718, like Doran's.'

'And yours?' Kenna asked, holding her breath as she met Mr Dunbar's gaze.

Please say it is later than May of 1719. Please.

'There is one from the eighteenth of March 1719.'

She closed her eyes and cursed.

'Kenna?' her mother asked, clutching her hand. 'What have you found?'

'I... I don't know, not exactly. This may be the

woman's last letter to this man. It is dated the twentieth of May 1719.'

'Read it to us,' Mr Dunbar instructed. 'Please.'

There was something in the way he said it that made her throat dry—some meaning far deeper than she understood that sounded a warning in her head—but she nodded anyway, picked up the letter and read.

"'I send this as a final plea. Do not ask this of me. Do not demand this of me. He is my husband and the father of my children. I will not kill him. I have not the stomach or heart for such brutality. It matters not how cruel he is, nor how forceful you become. I cannot and will not be a murderer. Do what you will, but this is my final answer. If you ever loved me, you will let me go without consequence and let the idea of us go...for ever. Iso.'"

They sat in silence.

'And then the letters stop,' Kenna said. 'Do you think something happened to her? It may have been the last letter she ever wrote. There is fear in her voice, dread. She sounded fearful, pleading.'

'We may never know,' Aunt Flora replied. 'It was over twenty years ago, lass, and we don't even know her full name or the man she was writing to.'

Kenna set the letters on the table and sighed in exasperation. Her aunt was right. Despite the fear and urgency she'd felt, reading that letter, the fact was they were in the past—far in the past. Discovering the truth behind what had happened to Iso was not really of great import.

Why they'd been hidden in a clock in their house was.

'Why would Father have kept these when he did not even know who they were to?' Kenna asked. 'What about them was so important that Father had to hide them…and risk his life and ours to deliver them to the Camerons?'

'May I?' Mr Dunbar asked, gesturing to the letter. He picked it up and handled it with great care, his eyes savouring every word on the page as he read.

Kenna was missing something, but what? Why would this man care about these letters at all? Were they more of a clue than she realised or was Mr Dunbar keeping something from her?

'Is there any indication of who they are written to in any of the letters?' he asked.

They each scanned back through their batch of letters. Everyone shook their heads except for Doran. 'In this one, she calls him "Donnie"—a nickname rather than given name perhaps?'

Her mother choked and started coughing. After the fit, she reached for the tonic Auntie Flora set before her, took a sip of it and righted herself. 'I must rest, my dear,' she said, coughing one more time. 'Especially with the reading to come tonight. I can hardly wait to see you.' She ran a shaky hand over Kenna's head and smiled.

Her mother was weaker today than yesterday, or perhaps she had merely worn herself out at the market. Either way, she needed rest.

'Aye. This can wait, Mother. Rest.'

Aunt Flora guided Dierdre back to her bed, and Doran rose from the table.

'I must be off,' he said. 'But I shall call in for the reading this eve. I would not miss it.'

Rolf looked up at the man and nodded. Some unspoken agreement flashed between the men, and Kenna wondered what they might be up to— or, more importantly, what Mr Dunbar was about. Before she could ask him, he rose as well.

'Perhaps they will help us,' Mr Dunbar said, gesturing to the letters. His finger lingered along the one she had read from, and a touch of longing entered his voice, as if he didn't wish to leave at all.

'I hope so. I wish we had the others that paired with them,' Kenna said. 'It would help us have a clearer understanding of their relationship and who this mysterious Donnie might be, even though no crests or clans are mentioned by name.'

'There may be more there than we realise. We will continue with them tomorrow after your mother has had a proper rest,' Mr Dunbar said, not meeting her gaze. 'I will see you for the village rune-casting this eve, Miss Hay. Until then.'

All afternoon Kenna mulled over her interactions with Mr Dunbar and his behaviour with the letters from the woman named Iso. He had handled the letters with great care and re-read them with intention. Was she missing the importance of the letters or something about Mr Dunbar? He was supposed to be her protector, but his role in uncovering the mystery of the letters and journal Father had left them as it related to her own mission had increased. He seemed invested in the outcome, somehow, but why? Did he have anything to gain other than fulfilling his contract and duty to serve as her protector?

Kenna worried her bottom lip as her mother brushed her hair, taking great care to smooth it out in long, flowing waves. 'I still do not know why you want to go through all of this fuss for a rune-casting, Mother,' Kenna said, despite how much she enjoyed spending such time with her. It reminded her of when she'd been a girl, and her mother would brush out her wet hair after weekly washes. Kenna had hated it then, but found she quite enjoyed the pampering now.

'I wish to see how your skills have grown, my love. I imagine you are more skilled than even your grandmother, who was incredibly gifted with the sight. She was so gifted people were often frightened of her abilities. They thought she was a mystic that could cast spells and magic upon them. She wasn't, but her intuition could not be faulted, and that bothered people. Some of them were unkind.'

'Why did I never meet her?' Kenna asked.

'She died before you were born but, oh, how she would have adored you. You have her nose,' Dierdre said, tweaking the tip of Kenna's nose, which made her laugh.

'What was her favourite rune?'

'Hmm, favourite...' She shook her head. 'I don't know. I never thought to ask.'

Disappointed, Kenna looked down at the new emerald-green silk satchel secured to her waist and began to turn the stones within it.

'What is yours?' her mother asked.

'I like Sowelo, the sun rune. The idea of always having light, energy and abundance in my future brings me contentment.' Kenna sighed, thinking of her favourite rune with its jagged S. 'I know the day shall be a good one when that appears in my cast.'

'I suppose I am not too surprised to hear that,' her mother said. 'But you know we cannot have all sun in our lives. There must be the opposite for us to appreciate the good and to grow.'

Kenna nodded. She'd had far too much disruption for her liking, but she'd not tell her mother as much. There was no need to quarrel or dredge up the past on a glorious evening such as this.

'Now, look at you,' Dierdre said, handing Kenna the looking glass.

When Kenna spied herself within the fine oval hand mirror, she stilled. Was that really her? Her face was glowing with the small amount of colour her mother had added to her cheeks and lips, and her hair was brushed out in long, wavy tendrils; the colour of soft amber rippled along it when it caught the candlelight. Small, blue glass bobs hung from her ears and a matching pendant hung from her neck. She was a far cry from the woman who'd come into the village yesterday wearing men's clothing that had been too big for her and covered in dirt and wounds. Her mother had even taken care of that: she had parted Kenna's hair on the other side, so the swooping tresses covered the wound on her temple.

She felt beautiful.

She *was* beautiful.

It helped to calm some of the nerves bubbling in her gut. While Kenna did rune-casting every day, to do so in front of people—especially those like Mr Dunbar, who knew little of the runes—made her uncertain. Would they understand? Would these people think her a mystic like her grandmother and treat her with disdain afterwards?

She sighed. She would never know if she never left this cottage. Perhaps stalling was an option.

'They are waiting,' Aunt Flora called. 'Let us go.'

So much for that idea.

'Come, come,' Dierdre said, taking Kenna's hand to hurry her along. Kenna fell in step behind her, grabbed the dark cloak they had found for her to wear and followed them out of doors.

It was a short walk through the village to the small cave where the people held their large gatherings. The cold chilled Kenna's face, but thankfully the wind had died down, and light snow fell in hushed whispers through the crisp air. The trio travelled in silence, side by side with their arms interlocked.

Kenna savoured this moment of walking between her mother and aunt, knowing well it might never be repeated. She wondered what Father would think of them now as he looked down upon them. She knew he would be smiling and have a small quirk on his lip at the sight of her so dressed up. She was not prone to making a fuss over her appearance, and he would have teased her relentlessly while pressing a kiss on her head.

A mixture of firelight and candlelight danced along the dark walls of the opening of the cave, and Kenna's nerves kicked up as they neared the entrance. She released the arms of her mother and aunt. 'Just do what you always do, Kenna,' her mother whispered. 'Pretend no one is here but you.'

How did one do that when there was a small crowd of people nestled within the walls of a cave that was far vaster than it appeared from the outside? She swallowed and fiddled with the ribbon of her cloak. At least twenty people were there settled along the stone benches and boulders that offered natural seating around the fire near the mouth of the cave. She scanned the room. Mr Adair nodded a greeting to her, and Mr Dunbar's intense blue gaze shot through her, sending heat to her core. There he was, being ungodly handsome, just when she needed to focus her energy and attentions most. Her reaction to him was becoming unnerving, and rather irritating, truth be told.

Just do what you always do. Pretend no one is here but you.

Kenna chanted her mother's words in her head as she returned gentlemen's smiles, settled into the area next to her mother and aunt, and pulled back the cloak from her head so the material could settle along the base of her neck. Slowly, she removed the white cloth from her gown sleeve and laid it out upon the ground, smoothing out any pocks or ridges with her palms. Then, she gathered the satchel of runes from her waist where it was secured with her mother's brooch.

She turned them over restlessly in her lap as she scanned the people within the space. Who would want their runes read this eve? So far, no one stood out to her, but rune-castings always surprised her. Soon, the crowd of people fell to a hush and her mother spoke.

'As many of you know,' she began, 'I have been long estranged from my daughter, but she is here with us now. My Kenna is a caster of far greater power than I, and she is here to help guide us as a village. If there are any who wish to have their future cast, speak now.'

Silence fell over them, and Kenna's throat dried. A moment ticked by and then another and no one asked to have their future cast. Kenna wondered if they had all set out this eve in vain. Perhaps they did not see her as worthy because of her age or perhaps they sensed her own unease.

'I will,' Mr Dunbar said, his deep voice echoing along the rock walls of the cave.

'Then, come, Mr Dunbar,' her mother said. 'Sit before her, so she can feel your energy.'

Kenna had never before done a formal rune-casting in public with a man other than her father, and the idea of having Mr Dunbar so close to her was unnerving even before he sat down. Once he did, Kenna had to remind herself to breathe. His knees were a whisper from touching her own as he settled on the ground before her, his crossed legs mirroring hers. His arms rested on his knees and his hands were clasped loosely before him.

He met her gaze and smiled. 'Do not worry, Miss Hay,' he whispered. 'I won't have any idea if you make a mistake. I've never done this before.' He winked and those around them close enough to hear chuckled, which helped her relax, and quieted her nerves.

She smiled back at him, grateful for the ease he brought to her with his kindness. 'I will need you to unlace your fingers and let your hands rest open and relaxed on your knees with your palms up—like this.' She gestured. 'It helps me feel you,' she said, then flushed, realising what she'd said.

Blast. Why had she said that?

A wicked smirk flashed briefly on his face before he reset his neutral pose. She pressed her lips together and took a breath to continue. The man was dangerous, and he well knew it, based on that smirk. She commanded herself to focus and breathed deeply to settle the heartbeat that fluttered in her chest.

Just do what you always do. Pretend no one is here but you.

'Find the question upon your heart you wish to have answered and hold it there in your mind in singularity, Mr Dunbar. Do so until there is nothing else you feel or want in your being but an answer to that question. Once you have your question in mind, tell me, and I will begin.'

Mr Dunbar closed his eyes, and she took that time to study him. His dark, wavy hair flopped over one eye, and the ends of it brushed the top of his jacket collar. His Adam's apple bobbed in his throat as he breathed in and swallowed, and he rolled his broad shoulders as he relaxed.

There was a dark cord around his neck she had not noticed, and she wondered what sort of a pendant or charm a man like him might wear.

He didn't seem like a man prone to sentiment, so whatever it was had to be important to him, and essential. The candlelight glowed against his skin, and she wondered what question it was that burned so deeply within him that she would answer. She prayed the runes would give him peace, as they always did for her. For some reason, his peace was becoming important to her. *He* was becoming important to her.

She swallowed hard as that realisation hit. He was becoming important to her whether she wished it or not.

After a minute, he said, 'I have my question.'

She nodded, closed her eyes and shook off the distraction that feeling such emotion brought her. She began turning the runes over and over in their pouch until the rhythm felt comfortable and steady. 'Once I feel ready, I will pour them out on the cloth without looking at them. The ones closest to you will be the answers to the question you seek clarity for, and I will explain the possibilities of what each means.'

'Aye,' he acknowledged softly, his knee edging forward and resting directly against her own. She sucked in a breath as she felt the energy of him flow through her, a powerful energy unlike anything she had ever felt at a reading. The pressure of it anchored her to this moment, and to him, and she felt light and effervescent, like a flake of snow falling through the night sky. She watched herself fall and, when she almost touched the ground, she opened the pouch and spilled the runes before him. She didn't open her eyes until she was sure each stone had settled.

She heard a small gasp rush through the crowd before it settled into silence again. Opening her eyes, she scanned the ground. She stilled. *Curses.* What she saw before him wasn't what she had hoped for, but her runes were never wrong. Now she would have to tell him what they meant. When she met his gaze, her hesitation must have given her fears away.

'Just tell me what they mean, Miss Hay. It is not your doing if they are bad.'

His knee pressed against hers again, as if he hoped to reassure her.

She nodded, took a breath and met his gaze. 'While there are no bad runes, Mr Dunbar, these reveal a possible setback in what you seek.'

He linked his hands together and leaned forward on his knees, as if preparing for the worst. 'Go on,' he said.

'There are three runes closest to you, so they represent possible answers to the question you hold most dear. The first, the slanted cross, hints at constraint. There will be delays in what you seek. You must face your fears to move forward.'

He nodded and his nostrils flared. No doubt, she told him exactly what he didn't wish to hear. She pressed her lips together, as that was the softest of the runes before him. 'The second, the I, is a symbol of standing still or ice. You must turn inward to find the clarity and answers you seek. Only you can free yourself from this block.'

He sighed. 'There is worse than those two?' he said with a bit of a chuckle, which peppered through the crowd behind him.

'And the last,' she continued without answering his question, 'is the slanted H, which is—'

He interrupted. 'Aye. I know this one: disruption,' he muttered, running a hand through his hair before looking down at his hands.

'Aye,' she continued. 'It stands for disruption, which could mean an interruption by an unknown force or destruction of some kind…'

She couldn't bear to say the last part, so he did it for her. 'Or death.' He met her gaze, and the intense blue focus sent a chill through her.

She couldn't look away or deny what he'd said, so she echoed it quietly. 'Or death,' she murmured. 'I am sorry, Mr Dunbar.'

''Tis not you, Miss Hay, but the runes. I shall find my way through,' he said, and his look made her believe he would.

He rose and settled back on the boulder as a small round of applause rippled around her. Soon another person from the village rose for a reading, and the night went by quickly as she completed one after another. Her mother even asked for one and, despite her nerves, Kenna obliged.

The hours passed quickly, and soon the casting was over. Her mother thanked everyone for their participation and rushed to hug Kenna once the crowd had dispersed.

'You were wonderful, and so skilled, my girl,' she said, smiling and pressing a warm kiss on Kenna's cheek.

Despite the joy and accomplishment Kenna should have felt, she was numb and drained from the evening. 'Thank you, Mother,' she replied. 'I had no idea how tiring that would be. I have never done so many readings at once before.'

She was a bit unsteady on her feet and her hands shook, so she nestled them in the folds of her cloak to hide them away. The last reading with her mother had especially shaken her and she was having difficulty leaving the emotion and feeling of the reading behind.

Her mother did not know what rune she had hidden from her, and it plagued Kenna deeply, but she could not bear to share it in front of everyone. For saying it aloud meant it might be real and true, and she could not have either. She refused to accept what the runes had shown her for her mother's future. For once, she wanted to block them from her being and knowing.

'Are ye coming, dears?' Aunt Flora called.

'Aye,' Dierdre replied and tugged Kenna's hand.

'I think I shall walk back alone, Mother,' Kenna answered. 'I need a moment.'

'Of course,' her mother replied, squeezing Kenna's hand before letting it go. 'Do not tarry too long. The snow will be picking up soon. I can feel it.'

'I won't,' she replied. She watched them go and, once their voices disappeared, she emerged from the cave, lifted the hood of her cloak, leaned her head back and stood, staring into the falling snow. Why was her life so complicated? Why had loss become a regular part of her life? Why could she not make it stop?

'Care for a walk?' Mr Dunbar said from the edge of the worn trail.

She bristled at the interruption, as if he had

been reading her thoughts. 'Have you been waiting for me?'

'Aye,' he said with a shrug. 'I did not want you to be alone.'

'How would you know I would be?' she said, lifting her chin.

He chuckled. 'I find I am beginning to know your ways, Miss Hay. And I am still your protector, am I not? Our journey together is not over.'

Our journey together is not over.

The way he said it made her believe their journey together had just begun, and for some reason she didn't mind that suggestion.

Unable to voice any of those thoughts, she walked towards him and accepted the arm he offered. Comfort was what she needed, whether she wished to acknowledge it or not. She slid her arm through his and allowed their sides to brush along one another, creating a sweet, aching friction as they walked in silence.

Chapter Eleven

Rolf sucked in a steadying breath as they walked arm in arm along the trail back to the cottages in the village proper. Miss Hay entranced him. He could no longer deny the growing attraction and intrigue he felt for her as each moment passed between them. While they had been at odds with one another at the beginning of their journey, their time here in this village had thrust them together in a way that surprised him and made him unable to think of little else than her.

'How long have you been able to…?' He didn't know exactly how to phrase what he'd just seen.

'Cast runes?' she finished.

He nodded.

'As long as I can remember. I cannot even remember a time when I did not have runes or know what the symbols meant. Strange as it may sound, I dream of them. They are always buzzing around in the back of my mind, like a dull hum.'

'Like music?' he asked, uncertain of what she meant.

She smiled and stared forward. 'In a sense. At times it is soothing and other times it is something I cannot seem to turn off but wish to. And then, when I have such a fleeting thought about wishing it away, I feel ungrateful. It is a gift to intuit as I do, and I do not wish to begrudge it. I know I shouldn't.'

'But you do sometimes, do you not?'

'Aye, like tonight.' She paused and faced him. 'I did not wish to tell you those things, to have those be the runes the universe gave me. I want more for you, Mr Dunbar, no matter what question it is that you hold so dear to your heart. I want you to have peace.'

'Perhaps peace is just not meant for me yet,' he said. 'You have a snowflake.' He gestured to her eyelash.

She attempted to remove it, but it clung to her long lashes and didn't melt.

'It is still...' he said, pointing to her lash.

'Can you get it?' she asked, and her eyes fluttered closed. Her mouth slightly parted.

Deuces. How he wanted to kiss her. She was so beautiful this evening, and his connection with her so strong after such a reading. He gently brushed the snowflake from her long, dark lashes with the pad of his thumb, commending himself for leaving it at that simple gesture.

'You are beautiful, Miss Hay,' he said, unable to keep his thoughts at bay.

Her eyes opened and a softness fell over her features. 'And you are a charmer, Mr Dunbar,' she added a moment later, with a smirk. 'And I am doing my best to resist your charms, despite how many there are and how fatigued I am this eve.' She bumped into his arm and shoulder and laughed before she slid her arm back into his.

He chuckled and tugged her to him. 'Then I will behave myself, although I find myself intrigued by you.'

'And I you, Mr Dunbar. But,' she added, clearing her throat, 'we are on a mission, one that must be completed, and I know well we will part company as soon as it is completed.'

'How do you know that with such certainty?' he asked.

'You will no doubt be on to your next commission, whatever it might be.'

'I have no further commissions or contracts at the moment,' he said, and sniffed, knowing full well he was playing havoc with the truth. He had no further commissions because he was no protector in the first place.

'You are a tease, Mr Dunbar,' she said. 'But I shall forgive it this once.'

'And next time?' he asked, unable to cease their playful banter.

'I will punch you even harder in the arm than I did yesterday.'

He laughed aloud, a deep, hearty laugh that felt so good and strong in his lungs. She joined in. Before he knew it, they were approaching her cottage, and he found himself shortening his stride to extend their brief time together.

'Tomorrow, I shall ask Mother and Auntie to decipher more of the rune-castings from that journal and look closer at all of those letters,' Kenna said as they slowed their advance.

'Do you think it will aid us in understanding their importance?' he asked.

She shrugged. 'I cannot say, but I hope so. It all doesn't make sense yet.' She met his gaze, the glass bobs swaying along the sides of her neck as she spoke, and it mesmerised him. 'Why would Father keep them? Without the other set, we don't really understand their importance. How did he know they even had any importance to begin with? And why did he make me promise to deliver them to the Camerons before February? What was so important about it all?' She sighed and removed her arm from his.

'Perhaps we are not meant to understand yet.'

'That sounds exactly like something my father would say.' She shook her head and smiled at him.

'Thank you for sharing your reading with me this eve, Miss Hay,' he said, letting his hand brush briefly against her own. 'You have a true gift.'

And he meant it. She had fascinated him this eve in all ways. Just as on the first day he'd seen her, Rolf knew he was in trouble and in over his head with Miss Hay, but unlike then he found he no longer minded. He was ready to dive into the unknown and be overwhelmed in the process. Especially if that unknown was the beautiful and bewitching Miss Hay.

'Goodnight,' he said.

'Goodnight,' she replied with a small wave before she entered the cottage and closed the door behind her.

After leaving her at the cottage, Rolf travelled

on to Doran Adair's, which had become his place of dwelling during their stay at the Lost Village. He prepared himself for the questioning he had come to expect every time he returned to the man's home. As he closed the door behind him, he heard Doran call out his first question of the evening.

'Did you enjoy your walk…with Miss Hay?' he asked as he came into the main room.

While Rolf could have denied walking with Miss Hay and the joy he'd had from her company, there was no point in doing so. Doran seemed to know the answers to half of the questions he asked, and Rolf wasn't attuned to which ones he knew the answers to quite yet.

'Aye,' he answered simply.

Doran leaned against the door frame, crossed his arms against his chest and frowned.

'Best you not take advantage. The lass has suffered mighty losses. Do not become one of her many disappointments.'

Rolf balked and removed his coat, thrusting it on one of the wall hooks. 'And a good eve to you too,' he replied, angered by the insinuation he would hurt her or take advantage. He wasn't that kind of man.

Doran didn't move but lifted his brow. 'Touched the truth, have I?'

'Nay. I would never take advantage. I admire her, that is all.'

With that, Doran barked a laugh. 'Now that is about as true as a horse's ass,' he said, pushing off the door frame and settling into one of the chairs at the table. 'I have eyes, Cameron. So does everyone else. The way you look at her is...' he searched for a word '...more than simple admiration.'

Rolf's temper was rising, but he knew he was being a fool to continue to deny his attraction to the lass. Perhaps Doran would have some advice, even if Rolf didn't want to hear it.

Rolf sighed and slumped into the chair. 'I cannot deny she is beautiful, and intelligent, and a puzzle. She is far different from any woman I have ever known.'

'You are intrigued by her; I understand that. But she is still your charge, even though you are a bold-faced liar and not who she believes you to be,' he told him. 'She sees you as her protector—be that first. Otherwise, neither of you will survive this mission of yours.'

The man had a point. Everything bad that had happened to them had been due to distraction—his distraction. If he wasn't careful, it might cost them both their lives. 'You are right,' he replied. 'I will try to remain more focused.'

'Now that that issue is still…unsettled…we must talk about this map,' he said, shaking his head. 'I borrowed it from the Hays this eve in hopes we could pinpoint some of the features, discuss ideas about reasons for their importance centuries ago, as well as now, and compare it to current maps in hopes of locating that mound they mentioned. Interested?'

'Certainly,' he said, settling in a chair at the table as they spread out the old and new maps and secured them with whatever weight they could find. Soon the maps were anchored with half-full tankards of ale, lanterns and a handful of heavy stones used as weights for hunting. Rolf stood back and studied the maps, looking for similarities and differences between each.

Doran appeared to be doing the same. They both stood in silence, analysing what they saw. Doran was the first to speak. 'Something is off, but I cannot decipher what it is. Can you?'

Rolf shook his head. 'Not sure. Is it the scale? Some features seem enlarged, while others reduced, but I can see no pattern in either. Miss Hay said her father made his maps differently. Perhaps this is just another way he did so. Maybe it is more than the compass rose that he personalised.'

Doran nodded. 'Very plausible. Could it be as

simple as enlarging those places and things he values more and reducing those he doesn't?'

Rolf walked around the table to the other side. After analysing the map, he shook his head and leaned forward. 'Nay. Come to this side and see for yourself.'

Doran came over and squinted, crossing his arms against his chest once more. Finally, he let out a slow whistle. 'The man was brilliant…and patient. This must have taken an age to craft.'

'I'd say so. Creating a completely inverted map that doesn't look as such… The man was a genius. Do you think his family knew he did this for all his maps?'

'I don't think so,' Rolf answered. 'While Miss Hay knew of the altered placement of the compass rose, she didn't mention that the map itself was inverted, like some illusion, and there would be no reason to keep it from me. We were using it to travel to find this place. No wonder we were so far off. The map needed to be turned *and* inverted.' He shook his head. 'Knowing this will make the rest of our journey easier.'

'Now we just need to decipher all the symbols on the map and determine the importance of the letters and rune-castings notated in the journal.'

'Is that all?' Rolf yawned.

'Aye. Better be ready for a late night.'

'I was hoping you wouldn't say that,' Rolf complained.

'And here I was, thinking Camerons were tough,' Doran muttered under his breath.

'No need to slander,' Rolf replied. 'I'm awake and ready to find answers.'

Chapter Twelve

'How long has she been sick?' Kenna asked the next morning as her aunt poured a freshly brewed tonic into a tankard. Kenna watched the steam rise, and the intense smell of herbs made her wrinkle her nose.

Aunt Flora ceased pouring and set the kettle back on the table. 'Almost a year now. Each day she seems a touch weaker, although having ye here has brought back some of her fight, lassie.'

'What does the village healer say?'

'I think ye know the answer to that question, dear.'

Kenna did, but she was reluctant to accept it. Every day she discovered more bloody kerchiefs, and her mother's hacking coughs were extreme once they set in. Why couldn't Kenna have more time with her mother now that she had found her? Why was life so unceasingly cruel?

'Take that to her. See if it helps,' her aunt ordered.

Kenna nodded, clutched the mug in her hands and went to greet her mother in her room.

'Good morn, Mother,' she said. 'I've a tonic from Aunt for you.' She set it down on the nearby table, and then perched on the quilted covers on the bed. She held her mother's hand and smiled. She was far paler today than yesterday, and most of the joyful light Kenna had seen in her eyes the night before was gone. She savoured the little that remained and smiled.

'How are you, my girl?' her mother asked, squeezing her hand.

'A bit tired from last night, but otherwise I am well.' And she was, except for the anguish of knowing her mother was dying. Except for that bit, she *was* fine.

'Do not be upset, my dear,' she said, as if reading Kenna's thoughts. 'I have had a lovely life. Knowing you are safe, and finally seeing the gifts you have, sets my heart and soul at ease.'

'But they do not set me at ease, Mother. I wanted more time with you. I should have had more time with you. Then and now.' Her pulse picked up speed and anger grew within her—anger at her mother, her father, the universe and everything in between.

Her mother nodded. 'Aye. You should have. That was our decision. We made it to protect you, yet here we are. The very thing we tried to protect you from you pursue, but that is life.'

'We are trying to piece all of it together, but we have much to still uncover. Would you feel well enough to help me with the runic symbols? I do not know all the ones I have seen in the journal.'

'Aye,' she said. A bit of excitement entered her voice. 'Bring it here. I will help you. It will distract me from the taste of that horrid tonic your aunt has made for me.'

She made a face and Kenna laughed, relieved to have moved from her anger to something into which she could channel her energy. She left the room and brought the book back to her mother. She set an inkpot and quill on the table, so she could make notes of her own on another piece of parchment. She didn't wish to crowd the old, brittle pages with her own markings.

'This eve,' her mother began, clutching Kenna's hand, 'I want you to do a reading for me here. Can you do that for me?'

'Aye,' Kenna replied, despite the emotion tightening her throat. She worried her mother was asking for her last reading to be from her, and the idea of it turned Kenna's stomach. She wasn't ready; she wasn't even close to being ready to say goodbye to her mother.

'Open to any page,' her mother began. 'The order may not be as important as we think.'

Puzzled, Kenna flipped to a page and began, showing her mother the symbols she did not recognise.

'Ah,' her mother said, partially sitting up, her eyes widening. 'I have not seen markings such as this in some time. These are old, very old. Gather that leather-bound book from the shelf,' she said, pointing to the small shelf that held her books. Kenna plucked the single brown leather book from its place and handed it to her.

'This was your grandmother's,' she said. 'It has all her notes on the runes. Some were her readings, while most were new symbols she added as she encountered them along her journeys, or rubbings of runic carvings she found in mounds, caves, tombs and the like. She always had this book with her, and she added to it all her life.'

Kenna sat back on the bed, held the small but mighty book in her hands and ran her palm over the soft leather cover. Its thick, sewn pages were impressive, and the cover distinctive, with its own runic symbols and depictions carved within it. There didn't seem to be a specific order to the symbols, so she flipped through the pages.

'This is truly amazing,' she murmured, studying the rubbings, notes, hand-drawn pictures and maps of places where her grandmother had found carvings. 'These are from all over Scotland. I had no idea she travelled so.'

'In the end, it was what killed her,' Dierdre added, her voice solemn and quiet with a note of stillness. 'Horse-riding accident along one of the roads she frequented near Melrose. One day she was alive and the next…' She shrugged. 'Taken from this world.'

'How old were you?'

'The same age as when you lost me.'

To know her mother understood her suffering made Kenna sympathetic but also plagued her. If she'd known what Kenna would feel, why had her mother still gone through with it and left her father and her? Especially when it hadn't protected her from anything.

'I still don't understand the importance of this journal and why you felt you needed to hide it from me,' Kenna told her, still running her hand over the cover.

Her mother clutched her hand. 'I have not explained all, and I know that. The politics of the Highlands are complex, and those carvings in that mound and the additional etchings in this book suggest that the boundaries of the lands there could still be disputed now. Such disputes between the Camerons, MacDonalds and MacPhersons over the resources in the mines, access to the lochs and rights to the most fertile land would end in bloodshed—great bloodshed. And I have not even translated all its contents. Your father and I made an agreement to let those secrets remain hidden. In a sense, we were afraid to continue.'

'If you were so afraid, why did Father send me to you now?' Kenna asked.

Dierdre sighed and rubbed her hands together. 'I'm afraid it may mean that we do not have the luxury of continuing to hide those secrets, especially if someone discovered what your father had. They may have killed him to keep those boundary claims secret.'

'But how could they have known he even possessed such information? Could he have let it slip somehow?' Kenna asked. 'And how does it relate to the letters that he hid with the journal? I still do not understand at all, Mother.' Her pulse raged. She was flustered and confused.

Her mother patted her hand. 'All in time, dear. But I am tired now. We will talk more later.'

Kenna started to object, but her mother squeezed her hand.

'Please. No more for now.'

It felt as if all her suffering and grief had been for nothing, and it enraged her, but Kenna swallowed down the emotion tightening her throat and blinked back the tears that burned the back of her eyes. She was unwilling to have her last hours or days with her mother be fraught with discord and upset. Finally, she nodded in agreement.

'Your grandmother created her own alphabet of sorts in the back of her journal. Use it to decipher the symbols you do not know. Perhaps you can finish what your father and I left undone. I will rest now, for your reading this eve.'

Taking the hint, Kenna gathered up the books, tucked her mother in her quilts and handed her the tonic, which had now cooled enough for her to drink. Quietly, Kenna slipped out of the room, closing the door behind her and cursing the day the letters and journals had ever darkened their doors.

* * *

Being away from Miss Hay most of the day made Rolf nervous at seeing her that evening, but he'd wanted to honour her wishes of letting her mother rest before the reading. The awful, repeated dreams he'd had the night before about his own mother, and the man in the library he could never identify, hadn't helped his mood either. He was restless as he followed Doran into the Hays' cottage.

He also couldn't help but notice the stagnant way the air moved, as it often did in the home of someone gravely ill. It set his body on high alert. Miss Hay's mother must be ailing even more than he'd first thought. His chest tightened. He should have ignored Miss Hay's request and been here for her today to support her, whether she wished for his presence or not.

The fire crackled in the hearth, and the smell of lavender and sage surrounded them. The chairs had been moved tightly around the small table so all of them could be seated during the reading. The women were nowhere to be found, and Doran gestured for Rolf to sit at the table, but he ignored his friend and remained standing. Every fibre in his being told him that all was not well, and he'd not be caught sitting if he was needed.

After a few minutes, Flora Hay emerged from the room. 'I am sorry. We had hoped Dierdre would feel well enough to have the reading out here at the table, but she doesn't. She has invited ye all to be at the doorway, if ye wish.' She dropped her voice. 'In fact, she has insisted on it—especially for ye, Mr Dunbar, since ye are a guest in our wee village.'

'If she is unwell, I do not wish to…' Rolf began before he was shushed.

'None of that,' she replied. 'Come. Kenna is ready.'

He and Doran exchanged glances before following Flora Hay to the threshold of the door. The sight of Mrs Hay stopped Rolf cold. The woman's health had turned for the worse, and he was as sorry as he could be to see it. She was pale, her skin almost translucent, and a sheen of perspiration beaded her forehead and upper lip. Miss Hay sat on one side of the bed, holding her mother's hand, and nodded a greeting to them.

'Ah,' Mrs Hay said weakly. 'Now, we may begin.'

Just as she'd done with him the day before, Miss Hay invited her mother to think upon a singular question and hold it in her mind. After a minute, she nodded, and Miss Hay turned the runes within the satchel on her lap. The turning created a calming rhythm, and Rolf wondered if that was the music Miss Hay had said she often heard in her head.

Then, without warning, she spilled the runes onto the same white cloth from the night before that she had spread out on the colourful quilt. She completed her mother's reading, and then her mother made a final request.

'Take a reading of your own, dear,' she said.

Miss Hay hesitated. 'Of course,' she replied, nodding to her mother.

She closed her eyes and, after a few moments of thinking upon her question, she spilled the runes out on the cloth once more. The settling of the runes was far different this time. Miss Hay leaned forward briefly, and for a moment Rolf thought she picked something up, but decided he must be mistaken. It had to have been a trick of the light. Why in the world would she disrupt her own reading?

Colour rose in Miss Hay's cheeks when she leaned back and began explaining the runes that had been cast. After she finished, the room fell into silence.

'Thank you, my dear,' Mrs Hay said as her daughter gathered up the runes into their satchel and secured it back at her waist.

'Of course, Mother,' Miss Hay replied. She stood and moved down to hug Mrs Hay and kiss her upon the cheek. 'I will let you rest. Call if you need anything.'

'Nay,' she replied. 'I shall sleep. Perhaps I will even dream of the runes. They feel close to me.'

Kenna stilled, her smile faltering for a moment before she recovered. She stood and faced the men in the doorway. 'Have you made any progress with the map?' she asked.

'Aye,' Doran replied. 'We have some questions for you, if you are ready for it.'

'Of course. And I will gather the books for us to peruse. Mother helped me with some of the symbols I did not know, and the rest may be in my grandmother's journal. It seems the runes are not from the Elder Futhark, which I use, but the mediaeval one. Thankfully, my grandmother made her own alphabet, or key of sorts, for the others in the back of her journal. I will use it to decipher as much as I can.'

'Futhark?' Rolf asked.

'Aye. It is the name of a type of runes. It is called such as the "F, U, TH" sounds are the first of the runes. They stand for abundance, strength and protection, in their simplest terms, and were the first alphabet of sorts.'

Rolf shook his head. It was overwhelming. Miss Hay was brilliant, and when she talked of runes she became a brighter, happier person. He revelled in the sight of how it had changed her melancholy of minutes before.

'Is that all?' he teased.

'It can also be read from left to right or right to left, which makes translations challenging, at best.'

Rolf stilled and laughed aloud.

She turned to him in confusion.

'I do not laugh at you, Miss Hay, I promise. Bring the maps to the table, Doran. Let us see if I am right in my thinking.'

Doran shook his head. 'If I did not know better, I would think you a man too deep in his cups.' He unfolded the maps and anchored them to the table with nearby tankards and a mortar and pestle.

Rolf's pulse picked up speed as he leaned over the table, analysing the features of the map that had continued to confuse Doran and him earlier that afternoon. As he walked round the map and read the features from right to left, taking note of the exact words from Miss Hay, he smiled and a relief he had not expected made him feel light on his feet.

'That's it, Doran,' Rolf said, slapping his hand on his thigh at the realisation Miss Hay's words had brought. 'Some of the runes read left to right and others right to left. The ones drawn on the map could be the same—the map is the same.'

'What do you mean?' Doran asked, moving closer to where Rolf stood.

'The features are turned and inverted,' Rolf said. 'So is the direction. What we believed north-west was south-east. What we believed to be the Highlands was the opposite.'

'And?' Doran asked.

'And I think I know where this mound may be.'

'Do you?'

'Aye,' Rolf answered with a smile, crossing his arms against his chest. 'And you…you are a brilliant star, Miss Hay.'

He met her gaze with the unbridled gratitude and care he felt in his heart, and she blushed under his praise.

And I wish I could kiss you, this very minute.

But he swallowed the words and gifted her a full smile, one that he hoped would show her his heart, until the day he could tell her the truth and show her exactly who he was and the deep affection he had blooming for her deep inside him.

'Where?' she asked a bit breathlessly, sounding as eager as he to uncover the truth.

'Outside of Loch's End on the border of the lands that hold the Camerons and MacDonalds.'

'Have you been there?' she asked.

Doran's features flattened and Rolf stilled. 'Aye,' he replied. 'Another commission brought me rather close to that very place.' The lie felt like sand on his tongue. Doran frowned at him.

'Then we shall go there,' she replied, 'on our way to Loch's End. Seeing those runes in person would be a glorious distraction in this rather horrid affair.' Her hands shook and she smoothed them down her gown.

'Are you unwell?' Rolf asked, his concern for her outweighing the momentary joy he felt at uncovering a piece of their complicated mission.

Miss Hay pressed a hand to her temple. 'Tired. Some fresh air will help; excuse me.'

Chapter Thirteen

Kenna felt lost after the rune-castings at her mother's cottage, despite the temporary joy she felt over Mr Dunbar's decoding of the map and discovering the possible location of the mound that had begun all this intrigue. Her head throbbed and her vision blurred.

Her mother was dying.

Her father was dead.

She was lost, tired and uncertain…about everything.

She blinked to bring some focus to her steps, as she headed out on the trail that led deep into the forest and ran parallel to the main village road, to get some fresh air and to clear her spinning thoughts. Anger and fear propelled her through the snowy night, and soon the cottages were out of sight.

Nothing remained but the quiet forest.

'Miss Hay,' Mr Dunbar called, running through the snow to catch up to her.

She paused, relieved not to be alone, and yet fearful of being with someone, even if it was only Mr Dunbar. Her emotions were everywhere after the reading she had done for herself that evening about their own mission to reach Loch's End. Kenna could not hide her confusion and disappointment at the runes she had seen. For once, the runes had frightened her in what they had not said.

She bit her lip.

Mr Dunbar fell into a silent and easy rhythm walking beside her, and Kenna's emotions began to subside.

'Wait,' he said urgently, his hand clutching her forearm to prevent her advance.

Kenna halted, her body stiff and uncertain, fearful at what might come next. Was there an enemy about, an animal trap at her feet? To her surprise, he leaned over and plucked a small white flower from the frozen grass. He examined it closely and a soft smile formed on his lips. He looked up at her with the wonder of a child and handed it to her. Kenna hesitated but finally accepted the small flower from him. The chill of it on her warm flesh sent a shiver along her spine.

'What is it?' she asked as she brought it closer to her face. She turned the delicate flower between her fingertips. It caught the light of the moon, and ice crystals glowed and twinkled off its petals, as if it were a star. She had never seen such a flower before.

''Tis a snowdrop,' he replied, emotion deepening the lilt in his voice. 'I have not seen one since I was a child. They were my mother's favourite. She said they were the strongest and fiercest of flowers because they can thrive in freezing conditions and aren't crushed by the snowfall.'

He tucked his hands into the pockets of his jacket and his jaw tightened. His eyes clouded as he studied her and the flower she held. The weight of loss tugged down his shoulders and Kenna understood instinctively how he felt. He was remembering his mother.

'When did she die?' she asked.

'When I was eight. It was sudden and yet not a surprise to me. I remember, when they came to tell me, I felt like I already knew the words that would fall from their lips before they said them.' He shook his head. 'It was strange. It still makes little sense to me.'

She smiled at him. 'Makes perfect sense to me. It is how the runes feel to me,' she said softly, still uncertain how he would react to her mention of them. 'The day my father was murdered, when the rune warned me of the disruption, I knew something had happened to him. Deep down I knew he was lost to me. I did not need to have anyone tell me he was gone. I knew.'

Mr Dunbar said nothing and her gaze dropped away. She turned. The gentle, warm feathering of his fingers along her bare wrist stopped her.

'I believe you are such a snowdrop, Miss Hay. Strong, unwavering and beautiful all at once.'

She faced him and let out a shaky breath. The heat and longing in his gaze and the utter belief in her was almost more than she could bear after what she had seen in the runes this eve. 'Let us hope you are right, Mr Dunbar. I cannot afford to be anything less, now, can I?'

Her words landed more sharply than she'd intended, but they served her purpose. She had to gain some distance from this man, this protector of hers that threatened and unnerved every part of her self-control.

His hand fell away at her response and she turned from him. She twirled the small flower once more before tucking it neatly in her bodice.

The sharp chill of the flower touching her breast sent a pang of shock and longing through her. She shuddered, closed her eyes briefly and then opened them. She had no other purpose now that she had found her mother than to fulfil her father's wishes to deliver the letters and book to the Camerons at Loch's End. Her desires had no place on this mission. It didn't matter what her heart or her runes told her. It didn't matter how her loneliness fell away in Mr Dunbar's presence. She would wilfully ignore them both.

'Kenna,' he said softly.

The sound of her name stopped her cold, as if the syllables commanded her body to cease its advance. He had never called her by her given name before, and she longed to know why he dared now. They had shared a kiss, but no more, and she had never invited such intimacies between them, despite how she longed for them. Part of her ached for his touch, his compassion and his care. It didn't matter that he was paid to watch over her.

She missed being loved. Part of her was desperate to have it back, but did she want that love from him?

He came to her. She didn't turn but held still in anticipation as she heard him getting closer by the soft crush of fresh snow beneath his boots. Soon, his hand slid around her arm, just above her elbow, and she held her breath. His body was flush with hers, and she could feel the heat and slight pressure of his lips against her ear. 'Please. Walk with me.'

Did she dare?

'Why?' she asked.

'I want you to stop hiding. I saw that you hid a stone in your palm from the others at your reading. What was it? And why would you hide it?'

She stiffened in his hold. How had he seen it? She had tucked it beneath her sleeve with such care once she'd seen it fall. She turned in his hold and faced him. 'How did you see that?' she demanded. 'And what business is it of yours?'

He smiled. 'I have sisters who are quite adept at hiding things from me. I have learned to watch and to see what is there rather than the distraction of what they wish me to see.'

He cupped her cheek. 'I am your protector...and I care for you beyond those duties. I want to know why you believed you needed to hide it from everyone. What did you see that you could not face, that you could not bear for us to see?'

Her shoulders fell. Tears heated her eyes and she dropped her gaze.

'Kenna,' he said softly, lifting her chin so he could look at her face.

'You have no right,' she began, but her voice and chin trembled. 'No right…to be so familiar with me.' She clutched his wrist.

He furrowed his brow. 'Is that what upset you?'

'Nay,' she said, tightening her hold on him. 'I do not wish to be seen sometimes, but you *always* see me. I cannot escape your gaze.' A tear fell down her cheek and her anger increased.

He let go of her chin. 'Do you not want to be seen?'

'Nay,' she replied. 'I will be a pariah. People will not understand if they find out just how much I can see. How much I know.' She wiped her cheek. Now that she'd started to confess her fears, she couldn't stop. He'd uncorked them, and now they poured out unbidden, one after another, like a rockfall.

'What is it you saw in that rune you hid?'

She couldn't say it aloud. It was too much to face. She sobbed and covered her mouth. Why could she not stop crying?

'Come. Sit with me,' he said, guiding her to a small stone bench nestled along the pathway. The cold of the rock grounded her despite how it made her shiver. He gently pulled the hood of her cloak over her head, letting his hand drift along her shoulder to rub her back in circles. It sent a sparkly warmth through her, and the rhythmic motion calmed her. Soon her hiccups faded, and her breaths evened out.

'Did you learn that from your sisters too?'

'Aye. And my cows.'

She laughed. 'What?'

'Cows need to be calmed too, sometimes. I find I'm good at it.'

'You are full of surprises, Mr Dunbar.' She sniffed.

He looked at her with expectation, and she knew he still wished to know what she had hidden from him and what fears plagued her. She removed her glove and retrieved the stone rune she had hidden up her gown sleeve. She covered it in her closed hand, still reluctant to reveal it. He wrapped his hand around hers and squeezed.

'No matter what it is, you are strong enough, Miss Hay.'

'Kenna,' she said softly, squeezing his hand back. 'I do wish you to call me by my given name, despite what I said before.'

He smiled. 'Then call me Rolf,' he replied.

She nodded and opened her hand. The rune glared at her. She shivered, seeing it again.

Rolf flipped it over in her hand, leaned closer and studied it. 'Am I missing something? There is no symbol.'

'Aye,' she replied. She stared out in the distance, her eyes seeing nothing and everything. Not knowing was a terror she had not known before.

'What does a blank rune mean?'

She shrugged. 'I do not know. That is the thing. It has no meaning but what you believe it does. It means something has not been worked out yet. I have never had one in my castings in an answer to my own question—never. And I have been casting since I was a wee girl.'

'And that is what terrifies you—not knowing?'

'Aye,' she replied. 'I asked for guidance on our mission to Loch's End and it was the closest stone to me. I fear it means the future of this mission is out of our hands.'

'Or that it is *in* our hands to do what we will with it. I see this as an opportunity to embrace rather than something to fear. *We* seize our own destiny, Kenna. It can be something beyond what is predicted in the runes.'

'And what if I don't want that?'

'How can you possibly know what you don't want if you don't know what your future choices are? No one knows what the future holds. It is what makes life beautiful.' His brow furrowed.

While she understood his words, the feeling of such uncertainty was foreign and uncomfortable to her. She clutched tightly at the folds of her cloak in her hands. Would she perish along their journey to Loch's End? Would Rolf? Would they even find these Camerons and be able to uncover all the secrets hidden within the journals, maps and letters they possessed?

And, when they did, what would she do next? Rolf would leave for his next adventure. The dread she'd felt when her father died crept over her once more. She would be alone—again.

'I cannot go if I do not know what will happen,' she said.

He balked. 'Will you give up now, after all we have been through and all you have lost? Why?'

'Because I am not as brave as you believe me to be, Rolf. Despite what you may think of me, I am no snowdrop.'

'Nay,' he said, taking her hand in his own, lacing their fingers together. 'You are, Kenna. You are a warrior worthy of any man. You dressed as a soldier to travel across the Borderlands with an army of men where anything could have befallen you.' His thumb rubbed the top of her hand, sending heat and energy through her.

'But *you* were there. *You* rescued me. I did not do that alone,' she said, staring down at the stark beauty of their interlocking fingers, his so much larger and more certain than her own delicate, fragile digits.

'But *you* left, planning to do it all alone. How many women would have dared such? I can count them on one hand.' He tucked a lock of hair behind her ear, the pad of his finger eliciting a trail of fire all the way down to her toes.

'Why do you believe in me at all?' she asked. 'You do not know me. Not really.'

His thumb stilled and he lifted his hand to cup her chin and meet his gaze. 'Perhaps I do not know all there is to know of you, Miss Kenna Hay, but I know…' he paused, his gaze dropping to her lips '…that with every day that passes I look forward to the sight, sound and feel of you more and more. I long to know you, every part of you, in any way that you will allow me to. Do you not feel the same?'

Her lips parted and she stared at his mouth, eager to feel the heated pressure of his lips against her own again. Heat flushed her face, and she knew she could not deny the attraction between them and the safety his touch and presence brought her. But could she say it aloud, as he had? Could she confess the longing she felt in her heart?

She crushed her lips against his instead, and he gasped in surprise before matching the ferocity of her kiss. She was aching, hungry, and desperate to feel alive, real and safe, and he was all those things just now. He was Rolf, Mr Dunbar, her protector. And, above all else, he believed in her and cared for her. With him, she wasn't alone in the world, which she feared as much as the unknown. She was desperate to feel something other than grief, loss and fear. She longed to feel pleasure and joy.

Their kisses deepened and she lost herself in the exquisite pleasure of being held and kissed by him. She turned to him and slid her arm under his coat, feeling the rippling muscle of his torso beneath the thin tunic and plaid. He pulled her closer and her leg slid between his. He moaned as she arched her back towards him, her breasts pressing against his chest, closing any distance between their bodies. His hand cupped her buttocks and pulled her torso closer, eliciting a fire between her thighs.

Her pulse raced and her urgency increased. While she had never lain with a man, she wanted to now—with him, with Rolf. She wanted him to be the one.

She tugged the tail of his tunic out of his trews and pressed her palm flat on his flesh before letting her fingertips explore his back. He gasped and pulled his mouth away. His eyes were hooded and his gaze smouldering.

'Kenna,' he murmured, letting his thumb caress her lip. 'We must cease. It isn't right. Your mother is dying and you are grieving. I cannot take such advantage,' he said and then chuckled. 'Despite how much I may wish to, I cannot. I would hate myself in the morn.'

'And what if I hate you in the morn for rejecting me when I am in such a fragile state?' she replied, kissing the thumb resting against her mouth and shifting closer to the bulge of manhood now straining for release in his trews. He emitted an agonised groan and pressed a hand on her hip to still her.

'I wish you could see yourself now,' he said, holding the side of her face. 'You are wild, free, unburdened and more beautiful than I can even fathom.' Sadness came over his face. 'And I want…' he paused '…and I want nothing more than to make love to you. But there are too many things you do not know about me…about the future. I do not wish to cloud those things for you. I want you to be ready and know what you are giving me and who you are giving your love to. And I want you to know who you are.'

'And who am I?' she asked, her lips trembling and betraying the emotion she felt.

'Whoever you wish to be, Kenna. You are a

blank rune too. You can seize whatever future you wish.'

'And what if I make the wrong choices?' she said, a tear falling down her cheek.

'Then you will make them, dust yourself off and keep going. You are so strong, but you must believe it too. I cannot believe it for you. You are that snowdrop. You can survive anything.'

Disappointed and angry, she shifted off him, stood and rearranged her skirts. 'You are mistaken, Mr Dunbar,' she replied, her tone cold and distant. 'I am no snowdrop.' She pulled the small flower from her bodice. She threw it to the ground. 'And definitely not yours.'

She didn't wait for his reply but turned and left, leaving him sitting on the boulder with a crushed flower at his feet.

Chapter Fourteen

Rolf stood before the Hays' cottage door. The gentle rays of the mid-morning sun warmed his face. Any other time, he would have believed a glorious day awaited him, but not today.

He took a breath to steady his nerves.

She needs you. Set aside yesterday. Set aside all your selfish needs and be there for her. You are her protector. Be her protector. Be the man she wants you to be. Be the man she deserves you to be.

He exhaled, raised his fisted hand to the door and knocked.

Moments later, Flora Hay opened the door, pressing a handkerchief to her nose, her eyes red and puffy from crying. Without a word, she nodded to Doran and him and waved for them to come inside.

Rolf's chest tightened at the sight of Kenna kneeling beside her mother as she lay prone on the very settee they had sat on days ago, telling stories about Kenna's childhood. Dierdre Hay saw him and gave a weak smile. 'Come,' she said faintly. 'There is much to discuss.'

'Mrs Hay, please rest,' he said, walking towards her. 'Do not trouble yourself.'

'Nay,' she said, shaking her head. 'Help me sit up,' she commanded, reaching out her shaky hand to him, which he grasped gently to raise her to sit. 'It is why I sent for you. There are more letters. I should have told you both sooner.'

'More letters?' Kenna asked, positioning pillows behind Dierdre Hay's head to aid her. 'Why did you not tell us when we spoke of them before? Why keep it a secret?'

'I was not sure. I was a fool. I almost died without telling you everything.' A tear rolled down her cheek. 'Forgive me.'

''Tis no matter, Mother. I love you,' she said, kissing her hand.

'What is the importance of the letters you speak of, Mrs Hay?' asked Rolf, pulling up a chair beside the settee. 'I don't understand.'

Dierdre Hay stared into the fire and paused, her hazel eyes shimmering and wide. Her gaze told him she was elsewhere now, deep in the overlapping folds of memory and time. His pulse increased with anticipation.

'It may seem strange to see me now and imagine it, but I used to be a beautiful young lass with much to offer and the whole world before me. I was intelligent, agile and hungry for adventure. Isolde Cameron and I—the Iso from the letters Bartholomew gave you—were the best of friends. We hailed from the same clan. She was a MacPherson before she married. So was I. We grew up together.'

Rolf held his breath as her words settled around him. His fingertips and toes tingled at the revelation. He could not move. He was desperate for her to continue, but he didn't wish to startle her, lest she stop speaking, so he remained still and said nothing.

'And, despite how much time and complications had come between us, and how wealthy she became after her marriage to Laird Cameron, it was me she trusted in the end,' Mrs Hay said, looking down at her weathered hands that she rubbed together slowly.

'She wrote to me and asked me to visit Loch's End long ago, and she gave me letters to take home for safety. A form of protection, she called it. It meant the world to me that she trusted me so, and when I showed them to your father he realised that, together with the journal we found in the mound, it all meant something more than we ever expected. And that, if we weren't careful in how we separated the information, Scotland would be bruised by it. Creating further strife amongst the Highland clans and unrest amongst the Camerons, MacDonalds and MacPhersons was the last thing we wanted to do.'

'Do you mean you possess the mates of the letters father discovered?' Kenna asked softly, the emotion in her voice lifting the ends of her words.

'Aye,' she replied, meeting her gaze. 'I should have told you, but I was so shocked when you showed them to me that day…' She paused. 'How they made their way to your father, I will never know. The chances of them being reunited after such a time is simply…' she shrugged '…astounding. It is almost as if the letters were meant to be brought back together.'

'And after all this time,' Rolf murmured. 'What an odd miracle.'

She met his gaze and nodded. 'Aye.'

Kenna sat back on the rug next to her mother with her legs tucked in beneath her, like a child awaiting the end of a story, which in a way she was…just as was he. He could hardly wait for Mrs Hay to continue. Rolf saw the old woman differently now. Not as the woman with information he must have, but as a woman who knew his mother. *Mother.* She would know more stories about her than Rolf ever could. She became a lovely beacon of hope to him, just like Kenna.

Kenna.

Rolf stilled and stared at her as she sat next to her mother. She was beautiful and kind and he was falling for her. He was also falling for the idea of them having something long after this whole business of uncovering his family's secrets was done. But he could not hold both of these women as beacons of hope in his hands, could he? By admitting his relationship with his mother, he would expose himself as a Cameron, and his lies and betrayal to Kenna.

And Kenna would hate him for it.

But, if he didn't reveal his relationship with Isolde, he would lose this connection to the past and he would never know what had happened to her. He had to know the truth about the letters, and why any of it mattered enough to kill for. Without knowing, would he ever be free? Would his siblings and their children ever be free? Would he ever have any real relationship with Kenna if he never told her who he was?

Nay. He had to tell her the truth of who and what he was: a Cameron and a liar. How she responded to the information would be up to her. He had to face the consequences of his actions, and he felt ready to. He braced himself.

'You knew my mother?' he asked, his voice raspy and uncertain, but full of anticipation.

All the women in the room stilled and turned their gazes upon him. Doran Adair closed his eyes and cursed under his breath, knowing full well Rolf's timing was atrocious, and he was making a horrid situation for everyone even worse.

But Rolf could not stop himself. He could not stop walking down this path now that he had set himself upon it.

'Your mother?' Dierdre Hay asked, her gaze assessing him. Her eyes widened in disbelief. 'You are a Cameron?'

'Aye,' he said, his confidence growing. 'I am Rolf Cameron, youngest of her four children and her second son.' Pride resonated in his voice.

Dierdre met Rolf's gaze and studied him. A timid smile formed on her lips. 'Ah. You have the same softness in your eyes, now that I look closer. I can tell you are her boy,' she said. She reached over for his hand and he clutched her cool, smooth skin in his own, linking himself back to his mother. His heart swelled in his chest.

'I met you once when you were very young, just before she passed,' she said. 'It was then that she gave me the letters. She had fears then, and she wanted more than anything to protect you all.'

'From what?' Rolf asked.

She shifted uneasily on the settee and frowned, letting go of his hand. She stared down at her lap briefly before glancing up. 'Audric MacDonald mostly. He is the "Donnie" mentioned in her letters. He was crazed by the end of their affair and was unable to move on from losing her, and then his wife. And...' She studied him. 'What all do you know of their past?'

He ran a hand down his face. Did he dare tell them? What choice did he have? He could not hold back now; it might cost him the truth. He let out a breath and the words came out in a rush. 'I know that he fathered my sister Catriona but that he does not know it.'

Dierdre nodded. 'Anything else?'

He shrugged. 'Is that not enough?'

She shook her head. 'Nay. There is much more between them. Isolde and Audric MacDonald were almost betrothed when we were young. They loved each other fiercely—too much, one might say. And Audric MacDonald was a different man then, softer and kinder. He had not fallen into such cruelty yet.'

She shook her head. 'But when the newly appointed Laird Cameron, your father, showed his interest in Isolde, her father demanded she marry him instead. The Cameron clan had more wealth and power than the MacDonalds; they always had. It broke her heart and Audric's, but there was nothing to be done for it.' She sighed. 'That started us on this path. I wonder what might have happened if they had married and she'd become a MacDonald. Would any of this have come to pass?'

'Do you think she would still be alive?' Rolf asked.

'You wouldn't be, if they had,' Kenna said flatly.

Rolf stilled. He could hear the hurt and anger in Kenna's voice, and he didn't want to face it, but he knew he had to. He lifted his gaze and met her glare. The passion in her glassy eyes was like the wildest of seas and the anger in her tight, pressed lips told him what they had was now fractured, perhaps beyond repair.

'Kenna,' her mother said, sending her a sharp look. 'Do not say such things.'

'Why not?' she demanded. 'He has lied to me

from our first meeting and I would like to know why. Care to tell me exactly why you have been lying to me, *Rolf Cameron*, if that is indeed your name?'

'I suppose I deserve that,' he answered, matching the intensity of her gaze. 'I knew you would not help me once you knew who I was. You told me you hated my family and the MacDonalds and that you blamed us for your father's death. You never would have let me protect you, let alone work with you to work all of this out.'

'And Father?' Kenna asked. 'Did you kill him?'

He balked, insulted by her accusation. 'Nay.' He pointed to his chest. 'I was the person he was supposed to meet. He had sent *us* a letter to let me know what he had found. He wanted my help, and so I went to meet him as promised, but I was delayed. I was late. Someone got to him before me.' He ran a hand down his face. 'And it is a regret I cannot undo. If I had been on time for our meeting that night, he might still be alive and all of this would be naught.'

Mrs Hay squeezed his hand gently. 'But I would have missed meeting you and seeing you with my Kenna. There are reasons the universe ties us together that we can never understand, and that is good with me.' She smiled. 'I know you will protect my daughter, and I am grateful beyond measure for that.'

Kenna scoffed. 'He will do no such thing. I am done with this mission of yours. It was built on lies. Did Father even know who you were when you saw him? How do I know you are even telling me the truth now? You have lied before.'

'He may be a liar about some things, Miss Hay,' Doran chimed in, 'but he did not kill your father, and his protection for you and care for fulfilling your father's dying wish is genuine. I can attest to that. I know a liar when I see one.'

Flora Hay chuckled. 'Ye knew well before any of us, did ye not, Doran?' She shook her head. 'Why am I not surprised?'

She pointed to the man. 'Kenna, this man possesses a gift for truth that is unmatched. If he says the man is to be trusted, then he is, despite whatever untruths he may have given to get ye here safely.'

Kenna objected, but her mother shushed her and patted her hand. 'There is not time for such anger, dear. Please just listen.'

'Aye, Mother,' she said and smoothed back Mrs Hay's hair. 'You are right. That can be dealt with later. Tell us of the letters—where are they?'

Mrs Hay smiled. 'They are hidden on the shelf

in my room tucked in the book on the geography of these mountains.'

Flora Hay laughed and dabbed her eyes. 'I always wondered why ye kept that book, as I never saw ye read it all the while ye were here, not once.'

Kenna rose, gathered the book and settled it gently in her mother's lap. Her mother opened it slowly and let out a breath as she flipped to the centre, where a batch of pages had been carefully cut out and a bound set of letters nestled within. They were tied with a light-purple bow, and Rolf smiled.

'Mother's favourite colour was that very shade of violet.'

'Aye,' Mrs Hay agreed with a nod. 'Had been her favourite ever since we were wee girls.'

Their eyes met and his heart pulled. How he wished he had more time to hear all the stories of his mother's life as a child, but there was no time for that now, despite how he longed for it. He would be grateful for what stories he would hear and savour them for as long as he could. Meeting Dierdre Hay had been a blessing beyond measure, and he would not begrudge it, no matter how fleeting it was.

Kenna gently tugged the worn letters from their snug hollow in the book. Rolf ached to hold them and read them, no matter what the contents were.

His mother had touched these letters and bundled them with that very ribbon. She'd gone to the trouble of giving them to Mrs Hay for safekeeping rather than burning them. They had to be important. They had to matter.

Kenna found him staring at them as she held them and, despite the anger he knew she still felt for him, she extended them to him without a word of chastisement. Her unexpected kindness gutted him, and he felt he didn't deserve her forgiveness at all. She was good, kind and gentle without measure, and he was a clumsy, foolish oaf prone to a singular focus at times, destroying everything in his path.

'Thank you,' he murmured, unable to say anything else as he felt the parchment in his hands. He loosened the ribbon and set it aside. Before opening them, he was careful to flip through them, being certain not to disturb the order. He scanned the wax seals that were still intact; they were all familiar, with MacPherson, Cameron and Mac-Donald crests. Most likely they were all from the three dominant male figures in his mother's life: her father, a MacPherson; her suitor, a Cameron, whom she later married; and a past lover, a Mac-Donald she'd been banned from marrying.

'I would start from the bottom. They are in

order.' Mrs Hay paused. 'Some of it may not be meant for a son to read,' she said. 'Do not say I did not warn you. If it's easier, Doran can read them, or Kenna.'

'Nay,' Rolf said. 'I have come too far to shy away from the truth now.'

'So be it,' she said. 'You will have questions, and I will answer them the best I can. Some...' she shrugged '... I still have no answer to. But perhaps, if you re-read the ones Bartholomew found after reading these, we will be able to piece together what even he could not.'

Chapter Fifteen

Kenna struggled to quell the turbulent emotions within her and focus on what she was reading. How many times she had attempted to read this one blasted letter, she didn't know. But she did know Rolf had lied to her about who he was, and her mother was on the verge of dying. She hardly understood anything any more. Since Hogmanay, her father had been murdered, she'd travelled across the country on a mission to fulfil a promise to him, and she had been guided by a man who had lied to her the entire time she had known him.

And worst of all, she cared for that man despite his failings. Her stomach clenched. Kenna questioned everything Rolf had ever said, and everything they had ever done. Heat flushed her skin at the memory of their kisses and how she'd almost made love to him the night before. What a fool she had been. At least he had not bedded her under the guise of such lies. Perhaps he possessed *some* shreds of decency. But why even pretend to be her protector at all? Why not just steal what he needed from her and abandon her? He was a Cameron, and had the power and means to do as he wished most of the time without consequences, wasn't he?

But here he'd stayed with her family and her at the Lost Village despite whatever urgent information they possessed between them. He'd taken part in rune-castings, asked her about her past, and listened and given time and attention to her mother and aunt.

She watched him as he read so intently, his brow furrowed, his gaze unwavering as he read each letter. His need to know every word on those pages was evident. He had not spoken a word since they had begun their task of analysing them, and some of what was on the pages was more than any son should know about his mother.

It was harrowing to read about the woman's complicated love affair with Audric MacDonald, while she'd also tried to dissuade Gerard Cameron from his attentions. Once paired with the letters her father had discovered, who knew what they would uncover? Especially when Rolf was driven, intensely driven, to discover the truth.

So intensely driven that there were probably more lies she had yet to uncover. She stilled and sat up straighter. Was his original story to her about why he had come to Melrose also a lie? Where did the truth in his story begin?

'You said you were meeting my father. What were you coming to see him for that day?' she asked, equally determined to understand the layers of his deception.

Everyone stilled their endeavours and looked up.

Rolf paused and met her gaze, setting aside his reading. 'The letters that you found hidden in the clock… Bartholomew wrote to my brother, Laird Cameron, more than once mentioning he possessed letters from my mother that were important to us, and that he wanted to help us by giving them to us before they fell into the wrong hands. He hinted that the letters were something we needed to see, and that we could use them as protection.

'My brother thought it might be all lies, or a trap set by one of our rivals or enemies. I thought it was information about my sister Catriona and more. I wanted to protect her by getting the letters from him, so we could at least know what secrets threatened us rather than being surprised once more. Even though my siblings did not wish to follow up on the matter, I did. I thought it might be important and help us unravel some of the secrets we are still trying to uncover about our parents and our past.'

'What kind of secrets?'

'If I knew all of that I wouldn't be here riffling through all of these old letters, would I?'

'Aye. I understand that part,' she said, frowning at him. 'But what are you so worried about not knowing? You read these letters as if they are a lifeline to something of great import. How long have you been searching for the answers to these so-called secrets of yours? Why do you even think there is something to be found, besides what my mother mentioned about altered clan borders and how that would impact the clans and their resources in the Highlands?'

He hesitated.

'I believe you owe me and the rest of us the truth,' she said, wishing she could punch him in the arm as she had before. It would make her feel a great deal better. She imagined doing it instead; it was not nearly as satisfying.

He ran his hands down his trews, as if he was mustering up the courage to begin. 'When I was young, my sister Catriona, known to us then as

Violet, was lost at sea and believed dead...' he said, then paused. 'Or at least, that was what our parents told us, but through luck, fate, divine intervention or whatever else you may wish to call it, we found her a decade later under a new name, Catriona. She was alive, and we were able to reunite with her.

'Since then, my brother, who is laird of the clan, began reading through our father's old ledgers in hopes of understanding what had happened to our sister. He followed the trail of information to the isle of Lismore and discovered the truth: that my parents had knowingly left her there, hidden her there in a sense. While we believe it was to keep Laird Audric MacDonald from finding out that she was his daughter, we can't be absolutely certain that was the only reason.

'I want to know the truth and uncover what else our parents were hiding from us. Now that my sisters and brother are married and expecting bairns of their own, I feel a fierce need to protect them. I fear... I fear any secrets unearthed by others might threaten their well-being as well as our clan's livelihood. And I can't abide that. They are my family. I must do everything I can to protect them.'

Kenna nodded. 'Such as lying to me?'

To her surprise, he met her gaze. 'Aye. Such as

lying to you. And I am sorry for it. I never meant to hurt you. I just wanted to protect my family. I knew you would not speak to me if you knew I was a Cameron. You told me so yourself. But, based on this letter, I think I may have finally discovered what happened to my mother and why Bartholomew took such pains to protect these and the contents of the journal. Your father may have helped end the agony that has plagued us…and plagued me…for so long.'

Her throat dried.

'Audric may have killed my mother when she refused to kill my father and marry him.' He shifted and swallowed hard before handing her the letter he held in his hand. 'Read it to everyone. Let us see if you all agree.'

She hesitated, but took it and read it aloud, trying to mask the tremble in her voice.

'My Dearest Iso. All that stands between us, our happiness and unifying our clans at last is your husband. Seize this moment when you and I can be together at last, united in body, blood and spirit. We can unify lands that were always meant to be together and the people within it.

All you must do is be brave and do as we

have discussed. Only a few drops and he will die peacefully in his sleep. That is all that separates us. I have enclosed the vial. You have one week. If I do not hear of his death, I will know you have abandoned me, abandoned us and abandoned the chance for a unified Highlands. Do not disappoint me. Otherwise, I cannot be responsible for what I must do next.

Yours, Donnie.'

The sight of the symbol of the daylight rune of Dagaz with its butterfly wings etched beneath his signature stole Kenna's breath. She met Rolf's gaze.

'The symbol on your ankle is here,' she whispered.

He met her gaze. 'Aye.'

'Do you believe it was Audric that carved it upon you all those years ago?' she asked.

The muscle in his jaw worked, and his features tightened around his mouth. 'I think it is a strong possibility, although I may never know for certain. I wonder now if dreams and memories I have of a day in the library, when I was a boy when I overheard my mother fighting with a strange man and interrupted them, was the day my mother died. I remember a man knocking me unconscious when I cried out to her.'

Pointing to the symbol on his ankle, he said, 'Perhaps this was a way for him to leave his mark on me—punish me for being there. For trying to save her...if he did kill her, which I now believe is almost a certainty.'

Doran Adair cursed under his breath.

'Such a cruelty even I could not have imagined,' Kenna's mother said softly. 'I am sorry.'

'As am I,' Rolf agreed.

After a moment, he reached over and squeezed Kenna's hand briefly before letting it go. She shivered from the heat of his touch.

'Kenna...' he began and paused. 'Thank you for helping me uncover these letters. Without you and your family, I would never have known about Audric's desperation to claim and unify our clans and the land within it, or his designs to have my father killed...and that he most likely killed my mother. My family owes all of you a debt that we cannot repay. And I am sorry for the deception. I never meant to hurt you.'

Her throat tightened and burned with the words she dared not say. She did not trust herself, not now.

The earnestness of his apology stole her anger,

and her eyes welled with unshed tears. To know what he suffered, what his family suffered and what she suffered now overwhelmed her. She cared for this man far more than she wished to, and she didn't want to be the foolish girl who had regrets after their mission was over and done.

Although, if she were honest with herself, she knew it might very well be too late to prevent such attachments. Rolf Dunbar had endeared himself to her. Now she needed to know if that was who Rolf Cameron was, or if it was all pretend, and he had kissed her to keep her compliant until he discovered the truth he sought.

She opened her mouth to ask but remembered they were not alone. The question died on her lips. She would ask him later when they were alone and when she might be more equipped to accept his answer, no matter what it was. Just now, she felt fractured and ready to shatter at any moment.

'I shall take some air,' she said, patting her mother's hand before she stepped out. Once outside, the cool, sharp air of the winter afternoon soothed her. She closed her eyes and took deep breaths until her heart slowed enough that her thoughts finally did the same.

'Better?' Doran asked as he approached.

She opened her eyes to see him standing next to

her. 'You must have been a fine soldier, Mr Adair. You have a silent approach that is commendable. I did not hear you until you spoke. If I were your enemy, you would have felled me without a breath.'

He nodded, tucking his hands in the pockets of his coat. 'My apologies. It is hard to shake off the patterns of the past despite how long I have been here.'

'How long have you lived here at the Lost Village?'

'Over five years now, before we even called it that. While it had always been a place where the lost came to hide after the fighting increased in the north, it became a refuge for those who needed a place to mourn their losses and recover. Then, those people never left, and it became the village it is now. I found I liked the peace of it. I had lost enough and grown tired of all the death and carnage of battle. I decided I wished to be part of building something instead. When they asked me to help organise and lead this village, I was honoured. Your mother and aunt were some of the first to accept me in earnest when I came here a lost and embittered man.'

'That does not surprise me,' Kenna said, smiling at him. 'They were always champions to those who needed it.'

He smiled and it softened all his features. He was an attractive man but reluctant to be seen. She understood that. She also respected it.

'Because of that, and the devotion I have to them, I want you to know that I am at your bidding. Whatever you need to complete this mission of yours for your father, I will provide.' He shifted on his feet. 'And, as much as you may not be able to believe it now, I do believe Mr Dunbar… I mean Mr Cameron…will do the same. Despite his initial lies to you, he wants to keep you safe and honour his word to you and your father while still protecting his own to his family. It is a lofty order.'

'While I do not doubt your loyalty, Mr Adair, I do doubt his. Knowing he lied to me so easily for so long and how taken in I was by those deceptions makes me ashamed.' Heat flushed her cheeks and she looked at the ground, crossing her arms against her chest.

'You should never be ashamed of giving your heart to someone, even if they do not deserve it.'

Flushed and flustered, she refuted his claim. 'I did not say I did such.'

He smirked at her. 'You did not have to. I can see it in the way you look upon him and the way he looks upon you, Miss Hay.'

'You are wrong,' she muttered.

'Then I apologise,' he said, holding up his hands in surrender. 'My soldierly skills of observation must be failing me. Either way, give him time, Miss Hay. You may find that his devotion has been genuine, despite the initial name he gave you. As a man of war, I understand the importance of deception for an end goal, but I do not expect it to come as easily to you. Promise me you will not give up on your endeavour to reach Loch's End just yet—for your mother's sake, at least.'

'But with all uncovered,' she replied, 'I do not believe I am needed. Mr Dunbar...' she began and then paused. 'I mean Mr Cameron has uncovered the truth he seeks, it seems. He has no further need of me.'

Doran Adair chuckled. 'He has more need of you now than ever, Miss Hay.'

She furrowed her brow at him. 'I do not understand you.'

He studied her face. 'Do you remember the first day you came to the village and I said you reminded me of someone?'

'Aye,' she replied, remembering the intense scrutiny of his gaze and how he had been arrested at the sight of her. She shifted on her feet, feeling shy about his scrutiny once more.

'Before I came here, I lost the woman I loved

to my own vanity and pride. I pretended I did not need her as desperately as I did and she left, uncertain of my attachment to her. She is lost to me now, and there is not a day that I do not despise myself for swallowing down my feelings and letting her go.'

Kenna bit her lip.

'Do not squash your feelings for him just to avoid the discomfort of revealing how you feel. Needing someone is no crime, nor is loving someone.'

Colour heated her cheeks. Then why did she feel so ashamed by it? She wanted to ask him but did not dare to.

'I do not mean to embarrass you by being so direct. I just want to spare you my mistakes if I can.'

'Thank you,' she replied. 'I will think upon what you have said, I promise.'

'I will return and leave you to your thoughts. Just do not take too long. Your mother...' He paused.

'Aye. I will be in shortly,' she answered, wiping a tear from her cheek. If she thought upon what he'd said too long, she would lose control and sob. Perhaps setting aside all her thoughts for Rolf was best for now. Her feelings for him were a distraction she couldn't afford. Kenna wanted to be present for her mother and enjoy the time she had left with her. So, she shook out her hands and promised herself she would not break. Not until she was good and ready and had the time to scream at the mountains until her voice was lost to the wind.

Chapter Sixteen

Rolf stared at the map spread out on the table, and turned it from side to side, trying to match the information he knew from the letters with the rune-castings Kenna had deciphered from the journal, and what he knew of the Highlands and the landmarks that might have been the same centuries ago.

'By all that is holy,' he cursed, scrubbing a hand through his hair.

'Going as well as last night?' Doran asked as he entered the small cooking area of his cottage and joined Rolf at the table. He yawned and Rolf followed suit. They had slept little the last two days in their quest to work out exactly where the mound might be along the border between the Camerons and MacDonalds and how to go about exploring the area without drawing undue attention or bloodshed.

So far, their hours of study had yielded nothing. It didn't help that every third thought Rolf had was about Kenna. Dierdre Hay had died during the night of their last visit, and Kenna had refused to see Rolf at all since then. Was she coping? Did she hate him? Did she wish to continue with their mission, or should he continue on alone to the mound and Loch's End? Was she reading her runes this morn? What did they say? Did she know how much he cared for her?

His heart squeezed in his chest. 'Why didn't I tell her sooner, Doran?' Rolf asked. Why had he not told her what he'd done to gain her help early on and then told her the truth before his feelings had grown, and before hers had as well?

'You didn't want to. It's that simple. You had opportunities to, but you took the cowardly way out.'

Rolf frowned. 'Thank you for the encouragement.'

Doran shrugged. 'I'm your friend. It's not my job to coddle you, but to tell you the truth. You behaved like a dolt. Now you must live with it.'

'I don't want to live with it. I want to undo it.'

Doran set aside the map. 'The best you can do is apologise properly. The rest is in her hands.'

'You are horrible at this.'

'But I am a master strategist.'

Rolf shoved him in the arm and laughed. 'Well, master strategist, do you agree with me that this area here is the most promising for us to search?'

'That looks to be right upon the border you share with the MacDonalds,' he murmured. 'Or on their lands. Neither would be good for us. It sounds like your families aren't on the best of terms.'

Rolf laughed. 'You are full of jests today. Nay, as you well know, we are not. If that mound is on his land, it will be inaccessible to us.'

'Perhaps to you, but not me. A night-time visit would not be out of the question.'

'Really?' Rolf asked.

'Aye. I am game, especially if this might turn the tables on the boundaries of the northern clans. I am curious to see if the rune symbols from the charcoal rubbing the Hays made from the walls in that hidden mound match those in the journal that Miss Hay deciphered. If they do, the Mac-Donalds will be losing more than land. They will have centuries of losses to undo. Reparations will have to be made.'

'Aye. The slate mines, access to the loch and the

lands they own that divide the Camerons from the Campbells will disappear and become rightfully ours once more.'

'It seems that not all of your parents' secrets were bad.'

Rolf scoffed. 'The irony is that *this* wasn't one of my parents' secrets. I do not believe they even knew. The horrid love affair between my mother and Audric led to this information, but it wasn't part of it.'

'But your mother kept the proof of MacDonald's plot to murder your father and join the lands, and she protected it, so you *would* discover it and be able to protect yourselves.'

Rolf stilled. 'Aye, but it makes me fear she might have died from doing so. Now that we know Audric wanted my mother to kill my father and marry him to join the lands back together, to *possibly* cover up his family's own secrets and deceptions, it makes me wonder if there may be even more to discover at that mound.'

Doran set aside the map and stared at him. 'What do you mean?'

Rolf sat down. 'The dreams I have about a man arguing with my mother and begging her to leave my father... I was in the library playing with a wooden toy when I made a noise and I was discovered. The man slapped me and I blacked out. The only thing I remember about him are the symbols on his wrist. And my mother died the very next day, or so I thought.'

'How?' he asked.

'A fall. They said it was an accident, but I always wondered if my father might have killed her. But now…what if Audric killed her to keep her silent about what she knew and about what he had asked her to do, since she didn't agree to it? What if he recently found out she had sent away the letters for safekeeping and is now trying to track them down to keep those secrets, and any others still hidden at the mound, from coming out?'

'Saints be,' Doran whispered. 'That is one hell of a theory.'

'It's also one hell of a secret. And I don't know what's worse—for it to be a theory or the truth.' Rolf scrubbed a hand down his face.

'The bigger question is, are you ready to find out?' Doran asked.

'As ready as I'll ever be. But, before we set out, I need to talk to Kenna.'

'While you talk with her, I'll rally some men and start preparing. If we leave tonight, we might just make it to the mound in two to three days if the weather holds.'

* * *

'Kenna?' Rolf called as he pushed open the Hays' cottage door. It squeaked open softly.

Flora Hay came out of the kitchen and Rolf went to her and offered a warm hug and his condolences for her loss. Before he could even ask for Kenna, the old woman pulled back, wiped her eyes and said, 'She is at the caves, dear. For once in her life, she is at odds with the runes. She is not herself. See if ye can help her. She will not listen to me.'

Rolf kissed the woman's weathered cheek, rushed out of the cottage and ran to the cave where Kenna had read his runes that fateful night which seemed so very long ago, despite it not even being a week since.

He stood at the cave entrance and saw her in profile, sitting in the same place where she'd read his runes. Kenna rocked back and forth with her eyes closed, as if she was listening to an internal rhythm or was deep in prayer—perhaps both. He wondered if it was the music of the runes turning in her mind. They were scattered before her on their simple white cloth and the emerald-green pouch that usually held them for safekeeping sat empty. He watched her for a moment, savouring the mere sight of her after not seeing her for days. When he took the first step into the cave, she spoke.

'I know you are there, Rolf,' she said, her rocking coming to a halt. She faced him and he shuddered. Tear tracks stained her cheeks and she was pale, too pale. This was not the Kenna he knew from days ago. He approached her slowly and sat cross-legged before her, just as he had done at his reading. Their knees touched and the contact sent shock waves through him.

Steady. He tried to think of where to begin. 'I am sorry about your mother,' he said, reaching for her hand. She allowed him to take it, and he shuddered at the chill of her cold fingers in his own. 'I am sorry about so many things, but most of all I am sorry I hurt you. I'm sorry I lied to you.'

He rubbed her hands within his own to try to warm them. When she said nothing, he asked, 'How long have you been out here? Your hands are freezing, Kenna. You need to go inside and warm yourself. Please; your aunt is worried about you. So am I.'

'I cannot,' she replied. 'Not until the runes tell me the answers I seek.'

He looked down at the spread of the runes before her. The blank rune she feared was closest to her. 'Is that why you will not go in—because the blank rune is still your answer?'

'Aye,' she said as a fresh tear streamed down her cheek. 'I cannot move forward. Not with that, I cannot.'

'But you can. This blank rune is a beautiful sign and opportunity for anything and everything you desire to come true, but you must choose it. The rune cannot tell you this time.' He smiled and squeezed her hands. 'It is setting you free to decide.'

'I do not want to make such a choice,' she said. 'And I do not want you telling me what I must do any more. You are no longer my protector,' she said. 'You are a liar.'

Her words stung.

'Aye. I'm not your protector any more in name, but Kenna...' he said, clearing his throat. 'I want to be more than that to you now. I love you. I think I have since I laid eyes upon you in those men's clothes that night on the stormy battlefield outside Melrose.' He chuckled at the memory. 'There you were in that terrible disguise of yours ready to take on the world, all to fulfil a promise your father made to a man you'd never met: me.'

Her hands softened in his hold and he continued. 'You are so strong, beautiful and intelligent.

You are absolute perfection to me. I want to spend my future with you, whether that is what is in the runes or not. Will you take that chance with me? Do you love me enough to try?'

Her gaze dropped from his and onto the scattered runes.

'They cannot tell you the answer this time, love. Only you can.' He held his breath.

Please say yes, Kenna. Be brave, say yes.

She slowly shook her head and let her hands slide out of his own. 'I am not the woman you think I am. I am none of those things to you or anyone. I cannot go with you, Rolf. I am sorry.'

'If I must accept that you do not wish to be with me, then I will, despite how it pains me. But I still owe you safe passage to Loch's End if you wish to see this promise to your father through. Doran and I leave tonight. If you wish to join us, meet me at the square at nightfall. If you are not there, I will know your choice.'

'You already know my choice. You made me choose it the day you introduced yourself to me as Mr Dunbar.'

Her words stung like a barb twisting within him. Knowing he could have prevented this by making a different choice all that time ago was a brutal reminder of why he did not risk his heart and why he dared not trust his feelings at all. It always led to ruin, as it had done with Joanna all those years ago when her rejection of him had been just as brutal.

He picked up one of the runes from the white cloth, sucked in a steadying breath and stood.

'If I could undo that choice, I would a thousand times over, because I find that I am nothing without you, Miss Hay. You are my transformation, my future…my light.'

He leaned over and kissed her cheek, pressing the familiar butterfly-design rune into her palm before he turned to leave.

Chapter Seventeen

'Pfft. Do not be a fool, lass,' Aunt Flora muttered, crushing the lavender and chamomile herbs with her mortar and pestle, while shaking her head. 'You have been puttering around this cottage for days.'

'I am *not* being a fool,' Kenna complained, tossing more lavender into the mortar to be crushed. 'I will not know what to do next unless I consult my runes.' She unpinned the satchel from her waist and opened the drawstring bag.

Her aunt set down her pestle and clutched Kenna's wrist. 'Nay. It is not the runes,' she said. 'It be ye, girl. Ye know what yer future holds; ye always did. Do not be afeared to seize it now. Stop moping about this cottage and go after the man. Rolf

Cameron loves ye. I know it.' She stared at Kenna and their gazes held. Kenna's heart thundered in her chest. 'And so do ye, despite those runes.'

'I am nothing without them,' Kenna said softly, fear coursing through her veins as she clutched the pouch in her hands. 'Even mother said so.'

The sting of her mother's death still plagued her. Despite being grateful for what time they'd had together, she was still tormented by it as well as another loss: the loss of Rolf. In truth, she felt paralysed by it far more than she'd ever expected to.

Aunt Flora let go of her wrist and ran a hand over her hair. 'Yer mother said no such thing to ye. The runes offer guidance, but the interpretation is yers and yers alone. It always has been. It is them that are nothing without ye. And the blank rune means *ye* have the power to choose, not the stones. But ye know that already.' She smiled at her and kissed her cheek before leaving her.

Something inside Kenna shifted and awakened within her. She stood frozen in the kitchen and blinked in the silence.

It is them that are nothing without ye.

Could that possibly be true? Could she be someone without them? Had she always been?

I find that I am nothing without you, Miss Hay. You are my transformation, my future...my light.

Rolf's words twisted free in her heart, and suddenly Kenna couldn't breathe. What had she done? The bag of runes fell to the floor and scattered. For once, she didn't need to look at them for guidance. She knew exactly what she needed to do and exactly where she wanted to be—with Rolf.

She did love him, as he did her. She had been a fool to think only the runes determined her future and her happiness.

She prayed it wasn't too late to find him. She ran out of the small cottage, spotted Doran Adair and rushed to him. When she reached his side, she grabbed him by the shoulder, interrupting a conversation with one of his men. 'Where is Rolf?'

'Why? What has happened?' he asked, alarmed, his body tightening as his gaze surveyed the area around them.

'I have been a fool and I must find him. Now.'

Understanding crossed his features and his brow softened. 'He is gone. After we found the mound, and discovered the rubbings your parents had found were true, he returned to Loch's End to tell his family of his findings and the additional journal there that we uncovered. I returned to the village after he set out on a different mission. Alone.'

'A new mission? I thought you said there was nothing more to uncover.'

Mr Adair dropped his gaze.

'Which way did he go?' she pleaded. 'Answer me.'

Mr Adair sighed but said nothing. She could see the war waging inside him.

'Please,' she said again, her gaze searching his own. 'Please. I love him. I must tell him. If something happens to him before I do, I…'

He cursed before giving in. 'He made me promise not to tell, but I am useless on such matters,' he said, ruffling his hair. 'He is headed west.'

'West?' she asked, puzzled.

'Aye. He has one more answer he seeks.'

'What is that?' she asked, her blood slowing in her veins. Her gut told her it had to do with his mother. That was the one answer they hadn't yielded. They hadn't uncovered what had really happened to Isolde Cameron, despite the theories they possessed.

Mr Adair's gaze turned serious. 'He believes Audric killed his mother, but he says he must know for certain, and there is no other way to do so than to confront him. He is taking on MacDonald on his own. He said he will not rest without the truth.'

Her hand fell away. 'And you let him?'

He chuckled. 'Have you met Rolf before? It was not a conversation, Miss Hay. He would not even take any of the men that offered to go along with him.' He looked down and then back to her. 'Not even me.'

'Fool of a man,' she uttered, before adding an unladylike curse of her own. The men could not contain the smirks on their faces. She frowned at them, and they stopped smiling. 'Well, I will take those men if the offer still stands,' she said.

He smiled broadly. 'Aye, it does. We shall be ready to depart with you within the half hour.'

She nodded. 'Thank you. He will be grateful to see us.'

Mr Adair shook his head. 'He will not be anything of the sort, as you well know, especially when he sees that I have brought you along.'

'Perhaps,' she replied. 'But he cannot take on a man like MacDonald on his own.'

'But that doesn't mean he's going to like it.'

'Rolf!'

Rolf stilled. *Kenna?* A mixture of terror and relief overcame him. He heard his name again, and he turned.

Saints be. It was her, here, looking down at him from astride a mare that had been ridden hard, sweat glistening off its coat. When he'd thought men had been pursuing him by horse, he'd been right, but it had been his friends…and her, who was so much more than anything he'd ever had in his life.

He didn't know whether to shake her senseless for putting herself in such danger or to rush to her and kiss the life out of her. He did neither and stood like a dullard until she dismounted, ran to him and threw her arms around his neck. Once the feel of her flush against him hit, he was helpless to resist. He hugged her tightly to his body, revelling in the sweet smell of her skin and the feel of the soft cocoon of her hair against his face and throat. He thought he'd never see her again, and in that moment he decided he would never, ever let her go.

But he would berate her for following him and putting herself in such danger. He kissed her lips and pulled back to study her face and make sure she was unharmed.

'Do not worry yourself,' she whispered. 'I am well. Now that I am here with you, I am very well. I was a fool. You were right: I do not need the runes to see my path forward…with you. I only need to listen to my heart.' The gentleness in her gaze and the soft tone of her voice calmed him.

'I could not stop her,' Doran called from behind her. He shrugged.

Rolf rolled his eyes. 'You are hopeless,' he replied to his friend. He tried to be angry but couldn't muster it. He was too happy to see Kenna to be truly angry with anyone.

'Aye,' he said. 'But at least I am equally helpful. I brought her here safely, did I not?'

He nodded. 'And I owe you a great debt for it.'

And he did. He loved this woman beyond all else and nothing else mattered. His heart skipped a beat. Well, almost nothing else mattered. He still had unfinished business with MacDonald. He would get the answers he sought from the old man for his siblings and their families, to keep them all safe. Then, he would be free, free of it all. Truly free to have and live a life with Kenna. Secrets would no longer plague him.

Kenna batted him on the chest and frowned. 'What exactly was your plan—to charge onto their lands and wage war against Audric MacDonald yourself? Alone?' She lifted a single eyebrow at him.

'Aye,' he answered, realising what an arrogant arse he had been.

'And was your plan to get yourself killed as well?' She frowned. 'We were lucky to have caught up with you so quickly. Mr Adair and his men are fine trackers.'

Rolf said nothing.

'Since we are here, what *is* the plan?' Doran asked, dismounting. He handed his reins off to one of the handful of soldiers that had accompanied Kenna and him and approached Rolf and her.

Deuces. What was his plan now? He'd thought of little other than barging in, demanding answers about what had really happened when he'd been a child, asking him about the bound book he had found at the mound with Doran and killing him—in that order, and without any difficulty.

He'd been a fool. Everyone looked at him with expectation. It was then he realised all their lives depended upon him and his choices in this moment. It was too much. It was always too much. He didn't want to lead anyone, because if he didn't lead anyone no one would be disappointed if he failed. But he also knew it was far too late to fear mere disappointment any more.

'There is still time,' Doran offered. 'You can send word to your brother and his men to support us and rally other men against MacDonald.'

Rolf shook his head. 'Nay. Bringing in many men will only escalate the chances for battle between us. My only hope is to just speak with him man to man, to get the answers I seek.'

'But Audric…is not an honourable man and he cannot be treated as such.'

'I will not risk anyone's life but my own.'

'But that is too high a price,' Kenna replied. 'Why do you wish to risk anything? Turn back; I am here now. We can build a life and a future of our own together. Is that not what you wanted, to move on?'

'I am so close to the end of it. To knowing all of it. How can I stop now?'

'And how do you even know he will not lie to you and then kill you when you ask if he killed your mother?' Kenna asked.

'I will get the truth from him. He will not deny me it. I deserve to know, we all do.'

'Why must you have this *last* answer? Why is what you have uncovered not enough?'

He stilled.

Why wasn't it? Why did he have to know all the answers?

'I don't know,' he replied. 'I just can't move on without it. Knowing the truth consumes me, especially now that I know there may be one more piece linked to the other book we discovered in the mound.'

He pulled the book from his saddle bag and showed it to her, rubbing the leather. 'This is a means to an end. I will use this as a bargaining chip with MacDonald to get the truth about my mother and the borders and what he conspired to do to my father.' He could hardly wait to confront the man. His pulse thundered at the thought of such a moment.

'Rolf, I beg you,' Kenna pleaded, clutching at the arm that held the ancient bound book so tightly. 'I beseech you, please…please leave this unknown. I do not want to lose you, not when I just got you back. And knowing this may not give you the peace you seek.'

'You don't know that,' he argued. His eyes were wide and his chest rose and fell in an irregular, jagged interval. 'I have come too far, lost too much, to settle for not knowing what happened to my mother and all the other truths hidden by him. How can you even ask me to leave this be?'

'I can ask you this because I love you and I love us,' she said. 'The answer you find will not bring us closer, nor will it help your family. The search for all of this has been nothing but poison. All the secrets, lies and deception to find the truth can stop here…with us.'

'I cannot.'

'Rolf,' she said, letting her hands fall to her sides. 'This last secret is *your* blank rune, and it is no different than mine.'

Chapter Eighteen

Kenna's words cut him to the bone, shattering the singular focus he'd had on confronting MacDonald, demanding he have answers about his mother and getting rid of this book he could not even decipher. What had happened to him in that library, and to his mother, had plagued Rolf for so long—too long. He looked down at the notebook he held as if it were poison. Was she right? Was *this* his blank rune? It couldn't be. All he wanted was the truth. All he needed was for the dreams and nightmares to stop.

'Nay,' he argued. 'It is not the same.'

'Why not?' she challenged, resting her hands on her hips.

'Why do you think it is?' he countered, still resisting the urge to see her reason.

'Because you desire the truth of the past so much that you cannot live for the present or for the future. You are trapped in the need to know, just as I was. I could not move forward with this mission and my life when I drew the blank rune because I could not relinquish control of wanting to know everything and predict every outcome in my future. When the runes did not guide me, and asked me to live by my own design, I was lost. I was frozen in fear and uncertainty, but there is no certainty to anything. You know this.'

'But, Kenna, I cannot pretend that this book is not here. It could change our lives for the better. It could give me and my family peace.'

She approached him and reached out, grasping his hand in hers, her face appealing and soft, pleading. 'Has it so far?' she asked. 'What has this quest for the truth brought your family other than misery? Did uncovering any of those facts about your sister and your parents' involvement in her disappearance or your mother's love affair make you stronger or happier? Is creating chaos and discord amongst the clans by sharing these new boundaries with them going to bring peace to the Highlands?'

'But this might,' he replied, lifting the book up to her.

'You are lying to yourself. You know nothing of the sort.' She let go of his hand and crossed her arms against her chest, her eyes flashing like bright blue-green sea.

'You are just angry because I will be able to complete my quest, and I will have answers about what happened to my mother that you may never have about your father.'

She blanched and took a step back, as if his words had punched her in the gut. Her eyes filled with unshed tears and she nodded. 'Perhaps,' she replied. 'But I will not be trapped in the past searching for those answers either. I will live my life and embrace my future. I can only hope you will come to your senses and do the same. Otherwise, this…' she gestured to the book in his hand '…is your future, and it looks rather bleak to me.'

She turned and walked away. She knew nothing of what this was, or what it would mean to his family's future and security of the clan. He ran his hand over the tattered bound journal.

What has this quest for the truth brought your family other than misery? Did uncovering any of those facts about your sister and your parents' involvement in her disappearance or your mother's love affair make you stronger or happier?

Her words rattled around in his mind and all he could think of doing was to go to his siblings once more and find out what they desired. They could decide as a family what to do with the truth, this book and Audric.

But first he had to tell them what he'd done by setting out alone, about giving up Kenna and what he'd found in this mound that he'd left out during his first reunion with them only a few days ago. He shuddered at the thought of how that meeting would go. They would be angry about his secrets and the peril he'd nearly placed himself in, just as Kenna had been.

While they knew that he had left to meet Bartholomew Hay in Melrose, and how that had gone sour, they didn't know he had pretended to be a protector to the man's daughter, anything about his feelings for Kenna, or about what disturbing this mound and the items within it might mean for them as a family and clan when he confronted Audric.

And then there were the letters. He cursed. They would also be none too keen to learn of the love triangle that had ensued between their mother, Audric and their father when they'd been young and later when they'd been married. Perhaps he should have just told them all when he had first returned, but he had been scared to admit the whole truth about what he'd done and the shame he'd felt about all the lies he had told to gain such facts.

He sighed. The only way to know what to do next was to face them and work this out as a family, just as they had a thousand times before. He rubbed the back of his neck, wrapped the old bound journal delicately in a swath of plaid and tucked it into his waist-belt for safekeeping. With his jacket over it, it was well hidden and protected.

To his surprise, Kenna waited with Doran and his men at a distance. They had not abandoned him yet. She and Doran were discussing something with intensity, based on their faces, and he knew well it was him. When Kenna caught sight of him, she broke eye contact and continued talking, ignoring his advance towards them.

When he reached her side, Doran spoke first. 'Miss Hay has apprised me of your plan to continue on.'

'Aye,' Rolf answered. 'I will take the book back to my family before I do so. I think it is something we should read together before approaching Audric.'

Doran nodded. 'Then I am in agreement with Miss Hay's suggestion to a change in plans.'

'And what is that?' Rolf asked, wondering what had changed so dramatically in such a short time.

'We shall escort you safely to the border of your lands. Once there, we will part ways. We will return to our home in the Lost Village and you can continue to yours. And the mission you both set out to do in honour of Mr Hay will be done.'

While Doran's reasoning was sound and his words true, Rolf didn't feel as if anything regarding Miss Hay was done. He had too much to say. This couldn't be the end of their time together, could it?

Something of what Doran had said echoed in Rolf's head. 'Wait,' he said, facing Kenna. 'Did you say you would be returning to the Lost Village? What of Melrose?'

'I will return there in time,' Kenna replied. 'But I wish to spend more time with my aunt, and grieve what I have lost properly.'

Was he part of the loss she would grieve? He swallowed, unable to ask that question, for he didn't want what had been between them to be over. He cared too deeply for her and longed for her to be a part of his life at Loch's End.

'Can we speak a moment, Miss Hay?' he asked, gesturing to an area a few feet away from the men.

'Nay, Mr Cameron,' she said. 'I have nothing more to say. You will not dissuade me from my feelings on that book or confronting Audric, nor can I persuade you to the opposite. We are at an impasse. Our time together shall end at the Cameron boundary once we reach it.'

There it was—the brutal severing he had feared.

'Miss Hay,' he said, but she would not look at him. 'Kenna.'

Her eyes flicked up to meet his gaze, but there was no reply.

'You cannot cast everything aside and return once we reach the Cameron border. Give me time to speak to my family. Time for them to meet you. Time for you to see Loch's End. You will love it. I know you will, and—'

'Nay,' she interrupted. 'I have wasted too long as it is being bound to the past and being fixated on controlling the future. I want to live my life in the present, and not be bound to fear any longer.'

'Shall you give up the runes?' He scoffed.

She lifted her chin and greeted him with a sharp, angular glare. 'Of course not, but they will not rule me as they once did. I will use them as a tool when I need them, not a necessity for living my day-to-day life, as I did in the past.'

'Shall you live this new life in the Lost Village, with Doran?' he asked, a flare of jealousy sparking within him. There had to be some other reason for her hasty decision.

'You are a fool, Cameron,' Doran growled. 'I do not dishonour her or you in such a way. It is you that dishonours her in suggesting such a daft reason.'

Rolf's face heated. Doran was not the type to betray a friend or to mislead a woman in his intentions. He was a soldier. He was disciplined, forthright and unfailingly loyal. Rolf was being a fool—again. He always was when it came to Miss Hay.

'Wait,' Rolf began, but Doran had already turned away and was assisting Miss Hay to mount her horse before pulling himself up on his own. Doran's men followed suit, and Rolf swung up on his own horse. He'd think while he rode. It would clear his head, as it always did. It was a few hours' ride to the Cameron border, and hopefully he would work out what to do before they reached it. Otherwise, this might be his last few hours with Miss Hay, and he couldn't quite abide the idea of it.

Rolf fell into the back of the line of riders and

watched Kenna's strong, steady, upright position and the smooth rise and fall of her body against the saddle as her horse began to gallop. How had what they felt for one another days ago faded into this? Would she really leave him at the border after all that had happened between them?

In his heart, he knew the answer: she would. Kenna was nothing if not resolved and strong in her decision-making once she'd set upon something. He thought of his first encounter with her during the chaos of battle, and how she'd demanded to know who he was and why, not accepting his first explanation readily. Despite his having saved her life, she hadn't instantly trusted him—although he had lied about who he was, so perhaps her first instincts were right.

Could she be right about this? Was he sacrificing his happiness and his future to know the secrets of his parents' past? Should he leave them dead and buried? The weight of the book secured along his waist reminded him of the importance of his decision with every gallop.

Kenna's cloak slipped off her head and rested at the nape of her neck, revealing long, loose, fiery tresses. Why did he have to choose between his family and her? Why could he not have both? He cringed. He sounded like his brother, unwilling to entertain the idea of being laird and being happy. The irony of such a revelation was overwhelming. He'd always believed he was vastly different from his older brother, but was he?

The hours clicked on without incident and the landscape became more familiar. The thickening of the trees along the ridge always reminded him he was close to home. But now would be the most precarious part, for they would pass a contested boundary of MacDonald lands. It was the smaller of the two MacDonald territories and was nestled against Loch Linnhe.

The front rider slowed and raised his hand in a fist, signalling the need to take heed and wait. Doran continued in a slow canter until he reached the man's side. They talked briefly. He and his men turned, and the line of riders followed, but Rolf didn't move.

When Doran reached Rolf, he stopped, bringing his stallion to a halt with a single *whoa*. 'We go no further,' he said. 'There are too many scouts. We won't risk Miss Hay's life just to bring you to your castle steps.'

Despite the ire in his voice, Doran gifted Rolf a smirk, which let him know there was nothing sinister in his remark and no ire between them.

Rolf nodded. On this count, he and Doran agreed. 'I understand. And I'm sorry for what I said to you.'

'Consider it forgotten. I will give you a moment,' he replied, and his men followed in tow, passing Rolf one by one. As the last soldier rode by, leaving only Kenna beside him, an unease settled upon Rolf. It felt like a final goodbye, and he didn't like it one bit.

'I have something for you,' she said softly. 'But do not open it until after I leave. Promise?' She extended a small wooden box to him, and it fit snugly in his palm.

'Did you plan to leave me then?' he asked.

'Blazes!' she cursed. 'Nay, I did not plan to leave you, but the gift was *for* you. It matters not to me that it shall be the last one. I just wanted you to have it, you stubborn oaf.' She murmured another curse under her breath and her horse neighed. She patted the mare's mane and cooed to her to calm her.

He was being an oaf, and he had no idea what to say. 'Do not leave, Kenna.'

'Why not?' she asked. 'There is no place for me amongst your past. I want greater things than to wallow in the sorrows of what I have lost. The odd thing is that I know you do too, yet you resist taking this leap. You are just as fearful, yet you call it something far more sinister.'

'And what is that?' he enquired, closing his hand over the wooden box.

'You call it being loyal to your family. You hide behind that crest of yours,' she said, pointing to the brooch securing his plaid to the shoulder of his tunic. 'It is becoming a yoke holding you back, as if you are a tree stunted by the oaks that grow tall and proud over you. Find your own spot to grow, Rolf. You deserve it.'

Doran whistled, and Kenna nodded to him. 'I must go. I hope you find the peace you seek,' she stated, and clicked her tongue to get her horse moving.

Rolf gripped her forearm and pulled her to him before she moved past, pressing a searing kiss on her lips. She kissed him back. When the kiss ended, he pulled away and released her arm. A tear glistened on her cheek.

'Goodbye, Mr Dunbar.'

Chapter Nineteen

Curses.

What could Rolf do now but watch her leave, like a dolt? He was a fool. She was the woman he had waited a lifetime for, if he were brave enough to admit it to himself. But to do so would be facing the truth: that he had ruined his chance of a life with a woman who knew him better than anyone else, and loved him anyway, and that he had no one to blame but himself.

He watched until they had disappeared over the bend before he turned his own mount and headed to Loch's End: home. It was usually a place of peace and comfort, and he had been excited at the thought of sharing it with Kenna. Had he believed she would come with him and not leave him at the border as they'd agreed? He had. Now he wondered why.

Why had he assumed she would be so charmed by him that she'd never want to let him go? It made little difference now what he'd believed: she was gone. He kicked his horse into a gallop. There was no reason to delay his arrival. He might as well charge in, explain to them what he'd found and decide the next step together.

He crested the final hill in record time. As the soldiers noted his arrival and recognised him, many cheered, happy to see his return. He was moved by the warmth of their greeting, and even more surprised to see Royce out on the grounds, walking. Rolf dismounted his horse and embraced him, more pleased to see him than he had expected.

'Brother,' Rolf said as they hugged one another fiercely.

'You are a sight,' Royce said, looking at him. 'We did not expect you to return to us so soon after your recent visit. Did you not return to the Lost Village as you planned?' His smile was wide and genuine, and he pulled him into an embrace once more, surprising Rolf. He still had not quite grown accustomed to this warmer and more affectionate behaviour in his brother, but he would not begrudge it.

'I cannot tell you how relieved I shall be for Susanna to cease her case for visiting you. She has been relentless.'

Rolf laughed deep in his belly. 'I would expect nothing less.'

'Come inside. Everyone will want to see you. I will have Cook start a meal and we will have a dinner celebrating your surprise return this eve.' He sniffed the air. 'But perhaps a bath is in order in the meantime.'

Rolf rolled his eyes. 'Fine. I will get cleaned up and rest and join everyone in the main room before dinner.'

'Two hours, brother: seven sharp. Do not be late.'

'Aye, brother,' he said in pretend annoyance.

'I must gather messengers to send word to your sisters to let them know you are here once more. Despite it being just a few days, you have been missed, brother.'

'I missed you too.'

A flutter of nerves captured Rolf as his hand paused on the door-knob of the drawing room.

Don't be ridiculous. This was his family and

his home. He had nothing to be nervous about. They would dine together and enjoy time with each other, as they always did.

I wish Kenna was here.

The thought came and went as quickly as a hummingbird, but he knew it was sound. He missed her, and he wished beyond measure that she was with him now, getting ready to meet his family for the first time. She was *supposed* to be here.

His heart squeezed. *Fool; you let her go.*

He had let her go. He had let her ride away from him when he could have done a thousand things to convince her to stay, but he hadn't. He'd let her go all for the sake of family and the unknown contents of a book. He only hoped it had been worth it.

He opened the door and they all turned. Susanna was the first to rush to him and she crushed him in an embrace while fussing over him at the same time. 'Your unexpected return has me overjoyed.'

He laughed and returned her hug. 'I am well, and it has only been a few days since I was home.'

He kissed her cheek and then pulled back to look upon her. She was glowing and happy, which set his heart at ease.

'And we have news of our own, do we not, Rowan?' she said, her eyes welling. 'We wanted to tell you a few days ago but were overwhelmed by your return and did not wish to cloud your arrival with news of our own.'

'What news?' he asked, gripping her forearms.

'I am with child. We are all expecting bairns at once!' she exclaimed. 'Can you believe it?'

Rolf stilled and emotion overcame him. He clutched her close to him, whispering in her ear. 'You see? It all happened, sister. You opened your heart, and look at your future now,' he said.

He looked upon her and found his throat tight with unspoken feelings. What if he had taken some of his own advice for himself, for Kenna? Would she be with him now, meeting the family he adored? He shoved away the thought with force. He blinked back the emotion he felt as Susanna wiped a tear from her eyes.

'I feared I would never have the chance to tell you.' She rested a hand on her chest. 'Silly, I know.'

'Aye. But you have, and now we have even more to celebrate. But first I must tell you the full truth of my journey to the Lost Village and ask for guidance about this...and Audric.'

He pulled the bound book from his waist-belt and set it on the table between two settees. His family looked at it and then back at him, and he commenced his full tale of his discoveries at the mound, the letters they'd uncovered, which he'd left out upon his initial return home days ago, and about his deceit with Kenna. Telling them about Kenna and leaving out his feelings for her was the most difficult, but he couldn't bear to share his heartbreak quite yet.

'And Miss Hay, Doran Adair and the other soldiers who escorted you along this journey,' Royce began. 'Did you not offer them respite here at Loch's End before they returned home? I would have liked to thank them properly for their service to us all.' He crossed his arms against his chest.

Rolf's face heated. He knew well what Royce was getting at, but he tried not to take the bait. 'They were eager to turn back. MacDonald scouts and soldiers were in a heavy presence along the area we planned to pass through. We did not wish to bring Miss Hay into any further danger.'

'Pfft,' Susanna said. 'Sounds like she can more than take care of herself.' She ran her hands rhythmically along the arm of the settee where her husband sat perched by her side. 'I am sorry I did not meet her.'

'And this book,' Catriona said, leading them out of the dangerous waters Susanna had brought them to by speaking of Kenna, 'may help us in getting the truth from Audric about what happened to Mother?'

'Aye.'

'But you are hesitant,' she said. 'Why have you not already opened it and read the pages for yourself?'

Why hadn't he? He had skimmed the pages but had not tried to decipher the runes and pictures within it. He merely viewed it as a bargaining tool with Audric.

'Because he does not wish to know any more,' Royce replied. He looked at Rolf. His older brother had a knowing look in his eyes Rolf had not expected. And he found, in that moment, that what his brother said was exactly true. He *was* afraid to unearth more for fear there would never be an end to their parents' secrets. Despite him believing this secret regarding his mother's death was the last to uncover, deep down he feared there might be more within that book. He shuddered at the thought.

'The answers I have discovered so far have not brought me the peace I hoped they would,' Rolf said, leaning back on the settee where he sat nestled between his two sisters, who were flanked by their husbands.

'There is not always beauty in the truth,' Royce's wife, Iona, added from the settee opposite them. Royce sat beside her and clutched her hand in his.

'She is right,' Royce murmured. 'My quest

for the truth about Catriona on Lismore has not brought us any peace. I should have left it undone.'

'But you would not have found me and I you,' Iona murmured. 'But he is right; it only provided more questions than answers. This book of yours may be the same, especially if Audric is involved in it.'

Catriona shifted on the settee. 'I still cannot fathom the love affair between our mother and Audric as young people, and later on, after she suffered the loss of the unborn bairn before I was born.'

'It is a great deal to take in,' Susanna agreed. 'How lonely our mother must have been to turn to Audric.' She shivered and rubbed her arms. 'I cannot fathom it.'

'You know how father could be, sister,' Rolf added. 'I am not as surprised as I wish to have been. Only saddened.'

'Aye,' his brother agreed. 'As am I.'

'Shall we burn it?' Catriona said aloud, sitting up and leaning forward. 'That way the truth dies here with us. The secrets will be over, and we can move on with our lives—set a new course as a family before these new Camerons, Campbells and Stewarts come into this world?'

Her husband, Ewan Stewart, kissed her temple.

'A fine idea. Letting go of the past has suited our family. Perhaps it shall be the same for you.'

Rolf thought of Ewan and how much he and his sisters, Moira MacKenna and Brenna MacLean, had been through after the passing of their father, Bran Stewart, and the new lives of beauty and hope they had built with patience and resolve. Surely the Camerons could do the same, if not better in their endeavours?

This last secret is your *blank rune.*

Kenna's voice echoed within him. She'd been right, as she always was, but Rolf had been too uncertain and unable to trust his own instincts. If he'd just stopped his search and left the book hidden in the mound to remain there for eternity, she might be with him now. He'd sacrificed their future, all for a book they would now burn anyway.

Curses.

'I agree with Catriona and Ewan,' Rolf said. 'What say you, Susanna? Brother?'

Susanna nodded, as did Royce.

'Since you have risked so much, it is yours to burn, brother,' Royce offered, gesturing to the fire.

Rolf hesitated and stared at the book, the itch to discover the truth beginning once more. He thought of Kenna. The sooner this chapter was closed, the sooner he could get on a horse and go after her. If he rode all night, he could catch up. All he wanted was to hold her in his arms once more and begin the next chapter in his future. A chapter he had set aside for too long.

He released his breath, stood, gathered the book from the table and walked over to the fire. He stood for long moments staring at the golden flames and the worn, decaying leather journal he'd found at the mound. Gathering a beat of courage, he lifted it directly over the flames and began a countdown in his head to release it.

'Don't!' Doran Adair shouted as he skidded across the wooden floor and into the room. His eyes were wide, and the usually reserved soldier was out of breath, his chest heaving with exertion, as if he had run a full sprint. The men in the room jumped to their feet, ready to counter an attack, removing the weapons every clansman had hidden on their person and settling into a defensive stance.

'Put your weapons aside,' Rolf said slowly, putting up a hand. 'I know him.'

The other men in the room relaxed their positions but did not take their gazes off Doran.

When Rolf pulled the book away from the fire and back to his side, Doran said a prayer and bent over, resting his hands on his knees as he tried to gather his breath. His hair flopped down to cover his face.

Gooseflesh pebbled Rolf's skin. 'What has happened?' he asked, his body thrumming in warning, knowing full well few things would put Doran in such a state.

After another long pause, Doran stood up slowly, and his haunted gaze told Rolf what had happened before he'd even said the words.

It involved Kenna, and he wouldn't like it one damn bit.

'He has Miss Hay,' Doran began, resting his hands on his waist and still clamouring for breath. 'And that book you found is what he demands in exchange for her safe return.'

'Who?' Rolf demanded, every muscle in his body tense.

'Audric MacDonald.'

Rolf roared a curse that echoed through the rafters of Loch's End, the fierce warrior in him unleashed. 'Where?'

'At the mound. He knows what you have found.' Doran shook his head and ran a hand down his face. 'I don't know how or why, but he does, and he knows of Miss Hay's gifts and...'

'And what?' Rolf seethed.

'And what she means to you.'

Everyone's gazes shifted to Rolf, but he ignored them. He would answer their questions about his relationship with Kenna later.

'How?'

'I do not know. Perhaps he had more scouts watching us along our journey than we realised. He must have had men waiting after we separated. They engaged us in a heated battle along the other end of their border, just when we thought we would be clear and entering Menzies land. These men were trained, very well trained. I do not believe they were MacDonalds.'

His implication was obvious to Rolf as well as the other men in the room.

'Mercenaries,' Ewan muttered under his breath.

They were the worst kind of soldier—at anyone's bidding for a price and without the complication of having a conscience. They were hired for their skills and paid handsomely for it.

'Aye. All of us were cut down, save me and one other man.' A muscle flexed in Doran's jaw. 'They spared us and ordered us to pass this message on to you. We rode hard to reach you as quickly as possible. Time is of the essence.'

He walked over and handed Royce a sealed letter. Rolf's brother had been eerily quiet, as had his brother-in-law Rowan. But both of their gazes were dark, and he could see their minds working at strategy already, just as was his.

Royce broke the wax seal with force and scanned the letter. His jaw clenched and he read through it once more before he set it on the mantel above the fire.

'Read it aloud, brother,' Susanna said coolly, lifting her chin in defiance. 'I will know the threats against us.'

'Aye,' Catriona chimed in. 'We all deserve to know. We are family.' Her husband, Ewan, squeezed her hand as she ran her other hand over her rounded belly.

Royce hesitated.

'Read it,' Rolf demanded, 'or I shall do it myself.'

His pulse increased and he clenched a fist at his side. He was struggling to hold his ground and not explode from the room to get to Kenna. His mind was racing with images of what might happen to her in the hands of a man like Audric MacDonald, but he also knew he needed to focus on the task of getting her back. Being flooded with emotion wouldn't help him to do that.

He needed to know everything about what had happened, what was in the letter, and they needed to formulate a plan. He could not race from here on sheer rage and chase the man down, despite how much he wanted to. He knew he would play right into Audric's hands, and he would do no such thing.

Royce nodded, picked up the letter and cleared his throat. Rolf noted the slight tremor in his brother's hand as he read, a sign that he was struggling to control his temper. It consoled Rolf to know they were united in the need to end Audric once and for all. Royce met Iona's gaze, and after a moment he looked away from her and began to read.

'Laird Cameron,
I have your brother's rune witch, and I shall keep her until he comes to the mound himself and provides me the book I seek. Then I shall cut him down in front of her and keep her for my own purposes to see if her gifts are as strong as they say.

My men will swarm Loch's End and remove the blight of your family from this land, my land, one by one—your bastard bairns in-cluded, save Catriona. I shall spare her until she has her bairn. Then, that babe will be mine, as she should have been all along as my daughter.

Cameron blood will flow across your land

like a river, washing it clean of your family's centuries-long betrayal and thievery. Then, MacDonalds shall reap the rewards of your bloodshed and build anew on this land.

My land.

Audric'

An eerie quiet settled in the room. A log split in two over the fire, sending a spray of embers on the carpet. Royce stamped them out.

'They shall be disappointed,' Rowan growled.

'Aye. They shall,' Rolf added. 'It is their blood that shall flow across these lands, not ours. Do not worry.' He gripped the hands of his sisters that flanked him on each side.

'I do not worry for us, my brother,' Catriona added. 'Just the innocents that may be caught in the midst of our battle.'

They sat quietly, not able to dispute her claim. Many would be lost if a full battle commenced against the sea of mercenaries Audric had hired to cut down everyone in their path.

'Perhaps it does not have to be a battle, but a beheading of the snake,' Rowan suggested.

Susanna looked at Rowan as he sat on the arm of the settee next to her. He met her gaze and rubbed her shoulder. Unspoken concern for him reflected in her eyes. Rowan had reasons for his hatred for Audric MacDonald. The bastard had killed his first wife and son years ago, and had almost cost Rowan his sanity, as well as his life.

Royce set aside the letter and sat next to Iona on the settee across from them. 'Aye. On this we all agree, do we not?' he asked, scanning the room full of his siblings and their spouses.

'Aye,' they each responded.

'Come, Doran.' Rolf gestured, as the man still lingered at the mouth of the room. 'Leave out nothing. This is our chance to burn Audric to the ground. For good.'

Doran Adair came into the room, settled in one of the open chairs and began. While the story about their battle with Audric's men and Kenna's capture was harrowing and hard to listen to, it firmed Rolf's resolve to cut Audric to the quick once and for all—and he had just the idea how to do it.

Chapter Twenty

Kenna's head slung back hard. Laird Audric Mac-
Donald's punch to her cheek had been unexpected
and it stung like the devil. She tasted blood in
her mouth, spat it out and blinked, trying to regain focus after the hit. The old man was unwell
and brutal, a lethal combination. She gathered her
focus and scanned the entrance to the mound once
more. It was still empty and dark with no hope on
the horizon.

He will come for me.

She knew it as much as she dreaded it. Rolf
wouldn't know to expect such a large group of men
within and surrounding the mound, especially not
at night. A cold wind blew through the opening,
and she shivered.

'Cold?' Audric asked with a snarl, his grey beard and long stringy hair making him even more menacing. He sneered at her while shaking her cloak in front of her. 'Read the runes to me, lass, and you can earn it back.'

'You can rot,' she muttered. 'I will read nothing for the likes of you.' She spat more blood at his boots.

'Tsk-tsk, young lass,' he said, circling her as if she were prey, where she stood tied to a stone pillar in the mound. His dark eyes raked over her body. 'You do not know what I am capable of, but your father does. One of my men took care of him.'

Rage flared deep within her gut and she struggled against the ropes, despite the pain of the cords digging in her flesh. 'Why?' She half-sobbed. 'He was no threat to you.'

'Nay, not a threat, but a thief. He had my box with Iso's letters, which was all that remained of her.'

'He was no thief,' she argued. 'A man sold him that box. I was there.' She pulled and groaned as she tried to free herself, but it was no use.

'But he bought it from a thief.' His eyes clicked up to meet her own. 'That is the same to me.' He shrugged. 'And, when he refused to return them to me, I had no choice. I could not have all my secrets thrust into the world, especially not into the hands of the Camerons.' He spat on the ground at the mention of their name.

'You will pay for what you did,' she warned.

He chuckled. 'No one cares about a lowly man such as your father, just as no one cares about you.' He clutched the shoulder of her gown with the intention of ripping it.

'Did you threaten Isolde like this?' she countered, hoping to stall his attack. 'Is that why she would never marry you? She knew how brutal you were, didn't she?'

His hand stilled and his eyes softened briefly at the mention of Isolde's name before reverting to their menacing glare. 'Do *not* speak of her,' he commanded, clutching the material of her gown tighter. Kenna winced at the pressure.

'I have read all the letters you shared,' Kenna continued. 'I know she did not choose you in the end but chose Gerard Cameron…and for good reason. He had more of…well…everything.' She hoped talking would distract him and give Rolf more time to reach her.

'She had her chance,' Audric continued, increasing the pressure of his hold on her gown. 'All she had to do was take care of Cameron and our lives…*all* our lives…and the future of the Highlands could have been so different. We could have been stronger, unified and more able to fight off the British.'

His eyes glowed, as if he were fantasising about a future he had imagined a thousand times without success.

She prayed Rolf's arrival would be soon. She shivered again, clenching her teeth as the wind bit through her thin gown and underclothes. Otherwise, she might well be frozen by the time of his arrival, or dead. Her bound hands were already stiff and aching from the exposure to the cold.

MacDonald laughed and let go of her sleeve. He shook his finger at her. 'I see your plan to distract me, lassie,' he said, wiping his eye. 'And it will not work.'

'Why not?'

'Because you're of no use to me dead.' He seethed and delivered another slap to her cheek. It stung less this time, but that might have been the numbness from the cold. 'You being alive is necessary to get what I want from the Camerons.'

'And what is that?' she asked, wanting to know what his plan was.

'Everything,' he said, followed by a long, deep laugh.

Her pulse increased. What did he mean? From

what Rolf had said, the Camerons had wealth and power that was unmatched by any other clan in the Highlands. How could this one man strip them of everything?

There was a muffled groan and then one of the soldiers who had captured her and thrown her atop his mount crumpled to the ground in the front of the cave, blocking part of the opening. She gasped.

Audric MacDonald smiled when he saw the dead man on the ground. 'It is about time, Miss Hay,' he said with a smirk. 'I do not believe you will like this next part, but I will.'

Another man shouted and then silence fell throughout the air.

'Here he comes,' Audric whispered to her.

Before she could react, the body crumpled in front of the cave was dragged away and Rolf appeared. The sight of him stole her breath. His face and forearms were smeared with dirt and blood, and his hair was wild and wavy. He looked primal and fierce as the moonlight cast a shadow around his form, just as it had that day in the fields.

But his eyes were Rolf's. He was there within the wildness of this being before her, and she had not lost him. He was there. He had come for her, just as she'd always known he would. It didn't matter that she had all but abandoned him hours before. He loved her, as she did him, no matter how they lied to themselves about their devotion to one another. Stubbornness could not sever what they had.

'Audric.' He snarled. 'Miss Hay has no part in this. Release her. Now.'

Audric laughed. 'Oh? As I expected, she has everything to do with our dealings, as she will make you more…cooperative, I think.' He pulled a blade from his sheath and shoved it into Kenna's thigh. She screamed from agony and then in anger.

'You bastard!' she shouted at him, panting and clenching her teeth.

'Breathe, Kenna,' Rolf ordered. 'Slow your breathing and pulse.'

She reached for the blade with her bound hands.

'No,' he commanded. 'Leave it in. Listen to me. No matter how much it hurts, do not remove it, and stay awake.'

Audric chuckled. 'Feeling more cooperative, Cameron?'

Rolf's gaze left Kenna and settled on Audric. His nostrils flared before he spoke. 'I am cooperative by nature, Audric. I brought you your book.' He removed a bundle from the saddlebags, which he then flung to the ground. Out of the bundle spilled a sea of letters, not a book.

MacDonald stilled and walked over to them. After he picked one up, he glared at Rolf. 'Where did you get these?'

'Dierdre Hay was most helpful. She gave us those. They were a bit more intimate than I was comfortable with, as it was my mother, but I wanted to know what your relationship was. Now I do.'

Rolf entered the mound as Audric opened one of the letters he had written to Isolde long ago. 'Go no further,' he commanded, still reading the letter, 'or I will pull the blade and let her bleed to death myself.'

Rolf froze.

Was this his plan? Surely not? If she removed the blade, she could free herself from the ropes that bound her hands in front of her and then cut through the ones at her waist. She glanced at the knife and her bound wrists, and then at Rolf. He shook his head, warning her not to do as she was thinking. How did he always know her plan before she did? She blew an errant tendril out of her eyes. It was irritating.

A glimmer of metal at the mouth of the cave caught her gaze, distracting her from her annoyance. Perhaps that was part of his plan.

'The book,' Audric ordered, tucking the letter in his waist-belt. 'I am out of patience.'

'I have it,' Rolf replied and threw the bound book onto the ground.

It slid and stopped at the tips of Audric's boots. He picked it up and smoothed his hands over it. 'Do you know what this is?' he asked with a wide, sickening smile.

'Nay. I did not read it.' Rolf pulled a dagger from his waist-belt.

Audric laughed. 'You are a fool, Rolf. Always have been. You are still the soft child you were when I met you, never willing to push too hard or risk too much. Do you remember our meeting in the library? On that day, I bedded your mother. She cried the whole time. She had lost a bairn, you see, and your father wasn't the consoling type, but I was. It didn't matter to me if she was married or not. But I do mind that she had already birthed a child of mine and never told me, and that the wee girl was hidden from me for decades. I *do* mind that.'

A muscle worked in Rolf's jaw, and he turned a dagger in his hand.

'What do you plan to do with that, son?'

'I am not your son.'

'No, you are not, and I am glad of it. You are too

weak, much like my own children.' Audric sighed. 'But I still hold out hope…for the unborn. Catriona's babe may have some potential. We shall see how she blooms under my care.'

'That will never happen,' Rolf countered.

'Oh, it will. Especially after I show all the other clans what rests in these pages, on those maps and in those letters. 'Tis the best-kept secret of the Highlands, you see.'

The man wasn't making any sense.

'And what secret is that?' Rolf asked.

'I will show you,' he said, untying the closures on the book. He opened the spine and flipped through its pages. His face dropped and he scowled. 'What did you do to this book?' he asked, running his fingers over the cut and torn pages. 'These are not the original pages. Where are they?'

'These pages?' another man called from the mouth of the cave. He was large, menacing and ready to kill. Kenna gulped. Perhaps she shouldn't have doubted Rolf's plan after all.

'Campbell!' Audric seethed. 'Finally, we shall have our time together at last.'

'Aye. So it seems.' He let the pages flutter to the ground.

Audric growled. 'I am out of patience, Rolf,' he muttered, rushing towards Kenna. 'And she is out of time.' He pulled the blade from Kenna's thigh and warm blood coursed down her leg. Her knees weakened and a lightness came over her.

'You bastard!' Rolf shouted as he lunged for the old man and tackled him to the ground. 'Did you kill her?' Rolf growled, his gaze settling once more on Audric's tattooed wrist. 'Did you kill our mother?'

Kenna spied the same butterfly scar she'd seen on Rolf's ankle on the man's wrist.

He laughed as they struggled. 'Took you long enough to work it out, Cameron. Fools, the lot of you. Aye, I killed her. She refused me and my offer to unite our clans by marriage.'

'She was already married.' Rolf seethed.

'But, as I explained to her,' he went on, 'she did not have to be. All she had to do was poison him—simple, easy. But she was soft...like you.'

He pulled a dagger from his boot and sliced one of Rolf's forearms. Kenna screamed, but her voice was muffled by the swords clashing outside the mouth of the cave, and then Kenna smelled smoke. *Fire.* She struggled to free herself as smoke billowed into the mound, but it only made the bleeding worse. She winced and stilled. She had to think of another plan.

Another man, about the same height and weight

as Rolf, rushed through the opening of the mound to her, his figure a bit blurry from the smoke and her dizziness. 'Miss Hay, open your eyes for me,' he said firmly. 'I am untying you. Once I do that, I'm going to carry you out of here.'

'What?' she murmured, unable to focus. She coughed on the smoke.

'I am Rolf's brother, Royce Cameron,' he continued, and wrapped something around her leg. 'I am sorry for what's coming next,' he said, and then cinched the fabric tightly around her thigh above the stab wound. Pain flashed hot and white through her, and she screamed.

'Got her?' Rolf shouted above the din and chaos.

'Aye!' his brother replied.

'Then, go. Now!' he commanded, elbowing Audric off his torso before the man he'd called Campbell dragged the old man away by his legs. They all disappeared into the billowing smoke.

'Rolf,' she murmured, unable to scream.

'Do not worry, lass; my brother-in-law Rowan shall take care of the old man. They have a score to settle that is long overdue.' Royce Cameron crouched down to carry her out from the smoke and tossed her over his shoulder.

'Why must all you Cameron men toss me about like bags of grain?' she mumbled. Soon they were out of the mouth of the mound, and she was being passed along to another man on a horse.

'She is conscious, but just,' he said, chuckling at her words.

'I will hurry,' a familiar voice said, cradling her against his chest.

'Doran?' she croaked.

'Aye, Miss Hay,' he said. 'I am glad you are still with us. Stay awake a few minutes longer, please. Otherwise, Rolf will kill me,' he teased.

She chuckled.

'Miss Hay? Kenna? Open your eyes,' Doran commanded.

'Nay,' she replied. The cold, black night pressed in on her and she finally let go.

Chapter Twenty-One

Rolf clutched Kenna's hands in his own and prayed. Why had he ever let her leave his side that day? He was so consumed by the past that he had nearly lost her and given away his future. He hated himself for what he had done. She had almost died because of him.

'Wake, please wake, Kenna,' he said, resting his head on her hands. Still, she didn't move. Days had passed since the battle at the mound, and yet she had not woken. He had sent for Bridget in Melrose in the hope some extra care from someone Kenna loved might help her heal. He'd slept by her side day and night, prayed more than he had ever prayed, and set her magical runes in her hands, hoping against hope that somehow their power would bring her back to him. He pressed a kiss to her hands and then rose.

He took the pouch in his hand and closed his eyes, embracing the soothing rhythm as he'd often seen Kenna do. After a few minutes, he opened the pouch and spilled the runes onto the top of the small wooden table beside her bed. When he saw the runes that had settled, he smiled.

Protection. Turning point. Partnership. Transformation.

All of Kenna's predictions for him had come true.

Now if only she would wake.

'Are you casting your own runes now without me?' she asked.

He stilled and turned to her. He rushed to her and covered her face in kisses. 'You are awake. You are alive. Kenna…' he murmured, nuzzling his face against her neck.

'And I am yours, lest you forget.' Her eyes welled. 'I love you.'

'And I you,' he replied, trying to sit on the bed next to her. He accidentally bumped her leg and she groaned.

'Sorry,' he said with a wince. 'Are you in much pain?'

'Aye. But less now that you are here.'

He clutched her cheek. 'I am so sorry that my

actions put you in such danger. Knowing the answers wasn't what was most important. You were.'

She covered his hand with her own. 'And Audric?'

'Dead. We burned the mound to the ground with him and all the secrets of the past within it. The letters, the journals, the books, the maps…they are all destroyed and shall be forgotten.'

'Even the land disputes?'

'Even that. It is not worth causing such upheaval for acreage. And I have great hopes for the new leader of the MacDonald clan. As I do for our future.'

'And?' she asked, and he knew what she wanted to know.

'He admitted to killing her. He was the brutal man from my dreams.'

'And the scar on your ankle?'

He shook his head. 'That may have to remain a secret unknown.'

She chuckled. 'And are you okay with that? With the unknown?'

'Aye, I am, and I have something for you,' Rolf said, pulling a small silk satchel from his coat pocket. He lifted her bare hand and opened it before placing the soft sapphire-blue pouch in her palm.

'Go on,' he said.

She tested the weight of it. ''Tis very light for a gift,' she murmured, before tugging the drawstring open and emptying the contents of it into her palm.

It was a rune.

She smiled and turned it in her hand. She turned it over again and laughed aloud. 'A blank rune,' she said with a smirk.

'Aye. The very one you gifted me when we parted that day.'

'And why would you give me back the same blank rune after I have almost died from an attack?'

'Because I hope our future is such: open to every joy, hope and possibility. Whatever you wish for in the world is yours, Kenna Hay, and I will endeavour to give it to you.'

'And I will endeavour to give you all you wish as well, Mr Dunbar,' she replied with a wink.

'Oh, back to calling me Mr Dunbar, are we?' he said, tugging her closer.

'I did like the reckless way about Mr Dunbar,' she replied. 'But I must admit, the name never suited you. I like Rolf Cameron much better.'

'And how do you like Kenna Cameron?' he asked.

'Hmm… I quite like it. More than I thought

I would,' she replied. He hugged her tightly and kissed her.

'Then it is yours, Kenna Hay, as is my heart. I love you.'

Epilogue

A month later

'Care to hold your niece, brother?' Catriona Stewart asked, cradling her sweet, beautiful bairn in her arms as she rested on the settee in the main room of Loch's End. She smiled at Rolf sweetly and glowed in her new role as mother.

Rolf's fingers tingled, but he stilled at the sight of the baby in his sister's arms. He was the last to enter the drawing room. All his siblings and their spouses were already there and had been there for some time this afternoon. For some reason, Rolf had dragged his feet in coming to meet the newest member of their family. Now that he was here, his heart pounded and his body clenched.

He didn't feel ready, and he didn't know why.

Kenna cupped his elbow as she stood beside him. 'Go on. You shall not break her,' she whispered in his ear. He could feel her lips curl into a smile against his lobe.

Rolf turned, kissed Kenna's cheek and stared upon his niece. The last few weeks had been a blessing, and he could not have been happier. He was no longer haunted by dreams of the past, nor by fears of the future. He slept peacefully in the arms of his wife, Kenna, each night and the demons of the past had been put to rest.

Even the clans of the Highlands had set aside their differences and begun anew with one another upon hearing of the passing of Audric. His death had left room for his son Devlin to grow into the strong but good leader he was meant to be, and for compromises and alliances between rival clans to be rebuilt. Catriona had even befriended her half-brother Devlin and half-sister Fiona, and built another bridge between their clans.

This wee babe in his sister's arms was but another reminder of the beauty of life, the unknown and the possibilities that lay before him if he dared be open to receive them. He walked over and sat on the settee next to his sister and Kenna snuggled in beside him. Rolf reached over for his niece and accepted her gently in his arms from Catriona. The light, feathery weight of the tiny babe shocked him, and he sat in awe as he soaked in the sweet smell of her skin and the vibrant blue hope in her eyes.

'This is Isolde Violet Stewart,' Catriona said.

Rolf couldn't speak. To know she had chosen the name of their mother as well as the name she'd been given before she'd been lost at sea and lived her life as Catriona shook him far more than he would have liked to admit. He swallowed down the emotion that threatened to overwhelm him.

'I did not wish to cast aside all the past,' she said softly. 'It is important to remember the best parts of it. Then we may cast aside what remains.'

'Aye, sister,' Rolf replied with a smile. 'And your wee girl is the start of all of that.'

* * * * *

COMING SOON!

We really hope you enjoyed reading this book.
If you're looking for more romance
be sure to head to the shops when
new books are available on

Thursday 21st
November

To see which titles are coming soon, please visit
millsandboon.co.uk/nextmonth

MILLS & BOON

MILLS & BOON®

Coming next month

THE LADY'S SNOWBOUND SCANDAL
Paulia Belgado

She hesitated, then straightened her shoulders. 'I've come to ask you not to evict the residents at number fifty-five Boyle Street.'

'Boyle Street?' He rubbed at his chin. 'Ah, yes. I purchased that building from a Mr Andrews...no, Atkinson.'

And it had been a fine deal as well, as Atkinson had been eager to sell to stave off his creditors. Desperate sellers always offered the best bargains.

'But why would I need to evict the residents? Isn't it some shop or factory?'

Lady Georgina's mouth pursed. 'I'm afraid it is not, Mr Smith. Number fifty-five Boyle Street happens to be St Agnes's Orphanage for Girls.'

'An orphanage? In the middle of a busy commercial district?'

She let out an exasperated sigh. 'You bought it, didn't you? You didn't know it was an orphanage?'

'I did not.' He frowned. While he had instructed Morgan to clear the building, Atkinson definitely hadn't mentioned there were any occupants, nor that they were orphans.

Damn.

'Oh, now I see!' She clapped her hands together. 'There was a mix-up then? And you really aren't evicting the girls?'

'I didn't say that.'

She blinked. 'You mean to throw over two dozen orphaned girls onto the street?'

Elliot ignored the knot forming in his gut and erased the vision of shivering waifs out in the cold her words had conjured in his mind. He'd made many cutthroat decisions in business before, and this one would be no different.

But his next move would no doubt be the most ruthless one he would ever make.

'I could change my mind. I mean, *you* could change my mind.'

'Me?' Her delicate brows slashed downwards. 'And what is it I can do to change your mind?'

'Marry me.'

Her bright coppery eyes grew to the size of saucers. 'I—I b-beg your pardon?'

'You heard me. Marry me and I will rescind the eviction notice.'

'You can't be serious.'

He was deadly serious.

Continue reading
THE LADY'S SNOWBOUND SCANDAL
Paulia Belgado

Available next month
millsandboon.co.uk

LET'S TALK

Romance

For exclusive extracts, competitions and special offers, find us online:

f MillsandBoon

X @MillsandBoon

⊙ @MillsandBoonUK

♪ @MillsandBoonUK

Get in touch on 01413 063 232

For all the latest titles coming soon, visit
millsandboon.co.uk/nextmonth

MILLS & BOON

THE HEART OF ROMANCE

A ROMANCE FOR EVERY READER

MODERN
Prepare to be swept off your feet by sophisticated, sexy and seductive heroes, in some of the world's most glamourous and romantic locations, where power and passion collide.

HISTORICAL
Escape with historical heroes from time gone by. Whether your passion is for wicked Regency Rakes, muscled Vikings or rugged Highlanders, awaken the romance of the past.

MEDICAL
Set your pulse racing with dedicated, delectable doctors in the high-pressure world of medicine, where emotions run high and passion, comfort and love are the best medicine.

True Love
Celebrate true love with tender stories of heartfelt romance, from the rush of falling in love to the joy a new baby can bring, and a focus on the emotional heart of a relationship.

HEROES
The excitement of a gripping thriller, with intense romance at its heart. Resourceful, true-to-life women and strong, fearless men face danger and desire - a killer combination!

From showing up to glowing up, these characters are on the path to leading their best lives and finding romance along the way – with plenty of sizzling spice!

To see which titles are coming soon, please visit

millsandboon.co.uk/nextmonth